The
FRIENDLY
Disaster

DINEEN MILLER

VINCI
BOOKS

By Dineen Miller

Seashells and Sunsets

The Desperate Deal

The Friendly Disaster

Messy Love on Mango Lane

Bloomed to be Messy

Rescued to be Messy

Tamed to be Messy

To Keith and Rachel…
yours is one of my favorite love stories.

Vinci Books

vinci-books.com

Published by Vinci Books Ltd in 2026

1

Copyright © Dineen Miller 2022

The publisher and the author have made every effort to obtain permissions for any third party material used in this book and to comply with copyright law. Any queries in this respect should be brought to the attention of the publisher and any omissions will be corrected in future editions.

A CIP catalogue record for this book is available from the British Library.
Paperback ISBN: 9781036709389

The EU GPSR authorised representative is Logos Europe, 9 rue Nicolas Poussion, 17000 La Rochelle, France
contact@logoseurope.eu

Chapter One

Prussian blue had to be a gift from the art gods.

Which said a lot considering she didn't care for most shades of blue. Even the blue of her own eyes could use a little Prussian blue so they didn't look so pale. But she adored shades of olive green, peridot, mustard yellow, burnt orange, rust red...

So many colors, so little time.

Emma Price dipped her brush into a small dab of the expensive watercolor she'd allotted herself for this project. Her salary as a part-time teacher at the art college barely made ends meet, let alone allowed for watercolor paint that ran close to twenty bucks for a small tube.

She supplemented by teaching private art classes at her art studio in a refurbished warehouse not far from Pineapple Avenue, which mostly covered her student loans.

The price for living in a beach town.

Totally. Worth. It.

She touched her brush to the watercolor paper she'd prepped and melted into the glorious gradation of color.

The deeper tones captured the blue jay's feathers almost to perfection, without having to adjust the color much at all. And though she considered her piece an abstract representation, she wanted to capture the essence of these fierce creatures.

Fierce, that is, to the squirrels who tried to steal their food from the feeder she'd hung from her small apartment balcony, and to any other bird trying to fly in for a meal. She could relate—she'd spent her lunch money on a tube of paint.

Again, totally worth it.

She sighed as she dragged the brush across the paper, building the layers of the feathers. The lighter areas had a gray-blue touch that still maintained the richness of the color.

"That was quite a sigh."

Emma jumped in her seat, which jerked her hand and left an obnoxious blue blob jutting from the feather she'd just meticulously painted. She growled and grabbed a paper towel to dab up the color before it set.

"Sorry. I didn't mean to startle you." Calen tucked his hands in the top of his jean pockets and slumped his shoulders. "That blue is intense."

"Prussian blue, and I love it." She caught most of the bleed, and could probably fix the rest after it dried. Watercolors were not as forgiving as acrylics and oils. "What are you doing here, Calen? How did you know where I was?"

"Because this is your happy place. Besides, Sheridan told me you'd be in your studio working today."

"You sabotaged my best friend?" She tossed the paper towel at the can and missed.

Calen picked up the wad and dropped it into the

garbage. "You wouldn't return my texts. Or my call. And what am I? Aren't I your best friend?"

She swished the paintbrush off in the nearby cup of water, dried it on a cloth, and then ran the bristles over her tongue to hold them together before she stuck the wooden end into the bun on top of her head—her way of keeping track of her brushes. Especially the small ones. Though sometimes she still forgot and found several stuck in there.

"Sheridan's my best friend, who's a *girl*. You're my best friend, who's a *guy*."

"Thank you for that delineation. I'm glad I'm still your *best* friend." He dodged her gaze, showing more interest in her painting.

Delineation? She hadn't heard that one yet. He must have spent the morning researching words for his poetry. "Just barely. After that performance last night, you almost slipped into the just-a-friend category."

The memory had played through her mind over and over. A perfect party to celebrate Sheridan and Noah's engagement. Singing karaoke with Manny, who'd seemed like a great guy. Super cute too. And a sous chef at Madilyn's Grill & Wine Bar. Then Calen's lunge at the platform, fist flying through the air and connecting with Manny's beautifully chiseled jaw. And down he went.

Manny, that is.

Calen had stood there looking like a misguided Viking. She had to say that seeing him that impassioned had surprised...maybe even impressed her at first, but then the horrific realization of what he'd done took over.

Now her chances with Manny were likely ruined, thanks to Calen's presumptuous attempt to protect her.

"I tried to apologize, but you took off." He fiddled with

her paint tubes, lining them up in a neat row so the labels faced upward.

"I'm not the one you should apologize to. Manny's the one sporting a sore jaw today, thanks to you."

"Did you talk to him?"

Did he sound hopeful or worried? She swiveled back to her painting. "No. I'm not sure he wants to talk to me after that debacle." There. She threw one of her own recent discoveries at him. *Debacle*. She'd had to look up how to pronounce it, though.

"Great word." He held his hands out. "I tried to apologize to him, but he'd left by the time I got back from trying to find you." Hands tucked back into his jean pockets, he shrugged. "I'm sorry. I thought he was that guy who dumped you last week."

"Well, he wasn't."

"Yeah, I know that now. Sheridan elucidated."

After an eye roll at yet another one of his new words, she studied him for a moment, this quirky guy she'd known since middle school. They'd shared almost as much life together as apart. She rose from her seat and rested her hands on his shoulders. "I know, and I appreciate it, but you really don't have to defend my honor, or whatever Shakespearean term you choose to call it. And I like the hair, by the way."

"Gets in my face a lot." He ran his hands through both sides to push it back, only to have it fall back in front of his eyes. He blew at it to make a point.

She touched the bottom of his hair just below his ears. "Just a little longer and you can tie it into a man-bun. Then you'll really look like a poet."

He rolled his eyes at her. "We'll see if I can stand it that lo—"

"Am I interrupting?" Manny stood in the doorway. His chef's jacket hung open, revealing a snug black T-shirt that tucked rather well into a pair of black sports pants. Better than she remembered from last night...

She'd better snap her chin back in place before she drooled. "Uh, hi!" The last word sounded more like a squeak toy. She cleared her throat. "Hi, Manny. This is a surprise."

Calen drew his brows together at her formal words. She sent him her signal that told him to back off. The one they'd established in high school to let the other know not to approach because they were in flirt mode. Calen said hers reminded him of a mad chipmunk.

Whatever, didn't matter. Just so long as he got the message.

Manny darted his gaze from her to Calen, then back to her. "Am I? Interrupting?"

She broke into a full smile and blinked—something she'd learned early on drew attention to her blue eyes even if they weren't dark enough to be considered compelling. "No, not at all. How'd you find me?"

"I asked Sheridan. Hope you don't mind. I really wanted to see you again." His voice lowered with his last sentence, sending a warm sensation through her. And he kept staring at her as if she rocked his world.

"Remind me to smack, then thank Sheridan." She said it more to herself than anything.

"What?" Calen and Manny asked at the same time, which made them frown at each other.

With a forced laugh, she waved it off. Why so nervous? Was she still breathing? Still standing? Her heart beat so loud in her ears that she couldn't tell. *Oh, no no no...not now.*

An anxiety attack would totally blow her chances with Manny. "I think I'll sit down."

"Breathe, Emma." Calen crouched in front of her, his face a blanket of calm concern. "Look at me and just breathe."

He knew better than anyone how random her attacks could be and how to help her head them off. But she didn't want him drawing attention to it either. She did what he said...deep breath...exhale...kept her eyes focused on the flecks of olive green in his hazel eyes. The tightness in her chest released and her breathing normalized.

"I'm fine, Calen." She gave him her look again. He was blocking her view of Manny. Dark and mysterious Manny, as she thought of and pictured him in her mind. He'd mentioned something about his father being Portuguese and his mother Italian. Made for the perfect mix of tall, dark, and handsome.

"Got it." He backed up a step and faced Manny. "Hey, about last night..."

Manny took Calen's place in front of her. "Not a problem. Sheridan explained everything." He didn't even look away when he answered Calen. Just kept examining her with that concerned expression.

Calen bobbed his head forward, which made him look like an awkward chicken. "Good. Still, I'm sorry I punched you."

Manny shot him a stern glance. "Like I said, not a problem."

The man should be on a magazine cover. How did GQ not know about him? Or some restaurant industry magazine? There must be one that he'd be the perfect cover material for.

He took her hand. "Are you okay?"

"All good. Thanks. Probably just dehydrated from my walk this morning." The warmth of his hand made her melt more than Prussian blue. That had to be something, right? Were they meant to be? She'd definitely sacrifice her pricey paints for this guy.

No doubt about it.

He rose to his full height, which turned out to be a few inches taller than her and almost as tall as Calen, yet his presence made him seem taller. The man knew how to fill a room. "What are you working on?"

"Oh, just a practice piece, really. Something I plan to demonstrate to my class." She lifted the pad. "Where is my paintbrush?"

"In your hair." Calen was still here? Why did he sound irritated? Didn't he catch her signal?

"I didn't know you taught too." Manny tugged it from her bun and held it out to her. "Can I watch you paint?"

"Of course!" She slid over on the seat and patted the space she'd made.

Calen's sigh came from somewhere behind her. "Catch you later, Emma."

"Later, Calen!" She tossed her reply over her shoulder, which brought her face closer to Manny's. His musky scent filled her senses and took her breath away.

She exhaled and gave herself a mental shake as she picked up her favorite paint tube. "This is one of my faves —it's called Prussian blue."

He'd give it two weeks. Three at the most.

Calen Cooper had a knack for predicting the length of Emma's relationships. Of course, years of practice had trained him well. Emma had a habit of falling for the wrong guys.

Shiny at first, then gone.

None of her relationships seemed to last long despite her intense desire for happily-ever-after. He had a theory why but kept it to himself. Any mention of Emma's father shut her down faster than a bad metaphor made him want to puke. Her real father, that is.

Calen had met the man only a few times when he and Emma hung out in middle school. Then her parents divorced, which started the panic attacks for Emma. Her father didn't know how to deal with them, so she saw him less and less until he finally stopped calling at all.

And despite having a fantastic stepfather by the time high school came, Emma never quite shook the rejection. Or the panic attacks. Over time, she'd learned to manage them better until they didn't happen very often. Only when she got overwhelmed or badly stressed out, but painting was her best remedy.

He wandered down the hall, passing several other artist studios. Felt bizarre not being at his coffee shop, but even business owners needed days off. And he'd promised himself that he'd work on his poetry today, which he did. Researched a list of words to add to his 'poetic vocabulary,' as Emma liked to call it. He preferred *expanding his mind*.

At the end of the hall, he turned into Maverick's Metal Studio, one of the larger units in an old renovated warehouse redesigned into various sized studios and marketed as 'workspaces empowered for the creative at heart.'

He hated bad personifications. "Hey, Mav."

Maverick stood over a large worktable with his welding helmet pushed up on his head, examining the tip of a welding torch. "Hey, Calen, what's up?"

"Came to check on Emma. Figured I'd come by and see if you have my order ready."

Mav gave him a questioning look. "I heard there was some commotion last night at Madilyn's."

Pineapple Avenue news traveled fast. "Heard about that, huh?"

"Yeah, heard you punched some guy out." Mav's grin of approval should make him feel somewhat vindicated, but it didn't. Just more of an idiot.

"Seems I punched the wrong guy."

After putting the torch down, Mav slipped off his heavy-duty gloves and leaned a jean-clad hip against the workbench. "She seems to pick the wrong guy a lot."

"Yeah, she has a type. Tall, dark, and trouble."

Mav's studious expression shifted into a lopsided grin, which raised his dark brow on that side.

Calen shook his head. "Don't even think about it."

He chuckled as he shifted to face his workbench again. "Don't worry. I don't date artists. Too much drama."

Such irony. How could he resist? "And yet, you are one." He flourished his hand outward for emphasis like a model at a cheesy car show.

"Not exactly. When your tool is a welding torch, you're considered a craftsman. Besides, I make practical stuff too. As you know." He leaned over the workbench and pulled up a metal display rack. "I followed your specs to the letter."

"Great! Thanks." Calen slipped out his wallet and pulled out their agreed amount.

Mav reached over again and lifted a rod that had hooks on each end and the word *breathe* in script, forming the middle. "And this."

He'd asked Mav to create the hanger for Emma's bird feeder. "That came out great. What do I owe you?"

"Fifty. You know, you could have just bought something like that for less."

"But then it wouldn't be an original."

Mav grabbed a magazine off the side desk and flopped it open in front of Calen. A picture very similar to the one Mav had made stared at him. And at half the price. "I used it for reference. See? Practical."

Calen pulled out more bills and handed them to him. "Yes, but this one won't say *Made by Mav*." He looked upward, imagining the label.

Mav screwed up his face like he'd just eaten a bad shrimp. "Dude."

"Yeah, that sounded way better in my head." But he did have a question. "Is Maverick your first or last name?"

No lopsided Mav-smile this time. "Yes."

Calen took a moment to process that one. "Okay then."

After stuffing the money into his pocket, Mav pointed at him. "You know, you would be a good fit for Emma."

He flattened his hands on his chest as he recoiled back. "Me? No way. We've known each other for too long. I had a crush on her back in high school, but that's ancient history."

"But you're the only one who seems to really get that girl, Calen. You gotta admit, she's a hot mess."

With extenuating circumstances. "But she's also super smart and creative. She just needs someone to complement her weaknesses, that's all. And protect her."

"Sure that's not you?"

"Trust me. I couldn't be more certain."

Chapter Two

The first glimmers of dawn promised a sunny day and the cool temperature a mildly humid one. Typical for Florida this time of year, as summer crept closer. Perfect beach weather too.

Calen read the sign displayed in the art gallery window. With the arrival of a major designer shopping mall a few years back, many strip malls had converted deserted spaces into art galleries. When the last place in this spot failed last year, the owners brought in a gallery to fill the space as a temporary solution. Who knew The Pineapple Avenue Art Gallery would become such a thriving success, giving their section of downtown Sarasota even more foot traffic and credence throughout the area? Even off-season, which they'd soon enter on the other side of Easter.

But this was a first—an official art show dedicated to local artists sponsored by two major art galleries in New York and LA.

Local artists are invited to submit portfolios for this prestigious show...well-known art critics...select pieces will continue to be featured in the NY and LA galleries...

He had to tell Emma. She should do this. She needed to do this. She *deserved* this.

And she would do it too, wouldn't she? Unlike him, who never went beyond publishing his poetry in neat little booklets he created on his own laser printer. And only sold them out of his coffee shop, which most who frequented Java Jerry's weren't really looking for poetry. Kaleena had sold a couple in her shop, Sass & Sun. Tourists loved her place even more than the locals.

Safe. That was his MO when it came to his art. But Emma...even in her messiness, she was fierce and bold. Two things he'd always loved about her. She should totally go for this.

Carrying the metal display rack and Emma's hanger he'd picked up from Mav yesterday, he crossed the street to his shop and went in through the front door. The early morning business crowd in need of caffeine would converge soon, leaving him just enough time to get this display up. He had a new line of teas he suspected would be the new rage with new agers and health nuts.

New rage with new age... The words danced into a rhyme in his head as he prepped the espresso machine and started a fresh round of coffee pots brewing.

So many words, so little time.

He finished setting up the tea display. The cardamon chai was his favorite so far. He read the packaging slogan again, "Time for tea and tea is time." Calen rolled his eyes with a groan.

A giggle drew his attention. How had he missed Emma's entrance?

"There's another revenue stream for you, Calen. Write better product slogans."

"Not on your life. That's why I opened this lucrative business of selling coffee and tea until I'm a famous poet."

"That's right. And when is that supposed to happen? Have you added it to your spreadsheet yet?"

He shot her a dirty look. "There is nothing wrong with setting goals."

She stood next to him and laid her head against his shoulder. "I agree, but goals can't be reached if you don't try. And they say if you write them down, you're more likely to go after them. Sounds right up your alley…writing things down. Did you submit to that poetry magazine you love?"

Her bun, which she called her blonde bomb, tickled under his neck. And she must have changed shampoo… patchouli and vanilla.

He grabbed a packet of chai tea. "I want you to try this tea and tell me what you think of it. I'll brew you a cup right now." He could feel her stare drilling into him as he darted behind the counter.

She sighed. "Fine, I won't push. But you know I'm right. You need to go for it, Calen. You're too good to stay hidden."

"Speaking of displaying your work, did you see the sign on the gallery window next door?"

"Are you kidding? It's all I hear about on campus. Even the students are discussing their submissions. There's going to be a lot of competition and a lot of grumpy students as the deadline nears. I am not looking forward to that. They're still hormonal teenagers to some degree. That's just adding fire to turpentine."

He smiled and pointed at her. "Nice imagery association there."

She gave him her best smile, the one that highlighted the light dusting of freckles on her cheeks. "I thought you'd like that one."

"Well, are you going to submit?"

She dropped her gaze. "Me? I don't know. Haven't really thought about it."

Her voice dropped as she spoke, which meant she was lying. And hiding.

"You were born for this, Emma. That gallery won't have displayed true art until your work is up there."

She did a laugh-snort combo as she looked at him. Her eyes held that glimmer of fear that going for it might come at a cost of her carefully managed peace and tranquility. "I guess I'll think about it."

He put a top on the to-go cup and slid it across the counter to her. "Promise me you'll think about it. And I'll help you with whatever you need so you don't get over-whelmed."

She gave him a noncommittal nod before lifting the cup and inhaled. "This smells amazing. Thanks." She glanced at her phone. "I better get going."

He called out as she headed to the door. "Let's talk more later. It's movie night."

She didn't look back as she pushed through the door. "Can't. Have a date."

He'd planned to give her the hanger he'd had made for her tonight. Guess that would have to wait, too.

What did she just read?

Emma flipped back a page and started the chapter again. At this rate, she'd finish the book next year. Maybe she should just give up. Her mind seemed more content to replay the story of her afternoon painting with Manny.

After glancing at her watch and noting the meager fifteen minutes she had left to soak in some sun to keep her vitamin D level up before her next class, she dropped the novel into her bag and relaxed, eyes closed, and let her mind explore the Manny Memories, as she liked to call them.

This mental album was filling up faster than the norm with cataloged details, too. She loved his smile. He swore he never had braces, yet every time he grinned, she thought of her zinc oxide paint and how much fun she'd have painting his gorgeous teeth. So white and perfect. And such a contrast to his dark complexion and black hair.

And his smell. Even through the lingering odors of the restaurant on his jacket, she caught the scent of his soap—lavender with a touch of patchouli. But then he took his jacket off, revealing a very well-developed physique—that she replayed a couple more times. How did he manage to look that good when he was around food *all the time*?

Breathe, Emma.

Calen's voice in her head interrupted the Manny Memories. She needed to take a breath and slow her heart down. Otherwise, she'd scare this one off, too. Just like the last one…*Chaaaarles*. The one time she had a panic attack while dating him, he'd told her to calm down. And not in a compassionate way. More like annoyed. She'd told him to have a wonderful evening dining alone and left the restaurant.

No surprise he didn't call her again.

She mentally pictured herself pulling that album off the shelf and pitching it into a large garbage can. And burning it. She laughed.

"What's so funny?"

Looking up, Emma cracked open an eye against the sun. Nina stood over her. Too bad she wasn't just a smidge taller so she'd block the sun about to blind her. "Just reflecting on the past."

Nina plopped down on the bench next to Emma, letting the tote bag on her shoulder slide to the sidewalk with a thump. "Is this day over yet?"

"I thought Mondays were your favorite day of the week?"

"I've decided to join forces with the world and hate them." Nina poked her bottom lip out for emphasis. "Everything was fine until they asked me to fill in for Professor Dumbledore."

Emma giggled. She loved the way Nina called the other instructors by movie character names. "Who's he again?"

"You know, Mr. Winston. He's originally from *Engggglaaand*. White hair and beard. Wears a funny hat sometimes." Her expression turned deadpan.

"I don't think I've met him yet. So what's the problem?"

"I don't enjoy teaching the fine art classes."

"But that's what your degree is in."

"Yes, but I like the film classes better." She let out a long breath and then smiled. "It'll be fine. What's new in your world, Ms. Price Is Right?"

Emma rolled her eyes. Nina spent too much time in TV land. "Oh, perhaps a Mr. Right."

"Seriously? You've only been dating that guy for like two weeks." Nina gave her a look of disbelief.

"No, not that guy. This one I just met. Well, kind of. I've noticed him before when I went into Madilyn's to see Sheridan, but then he started noticing me at her engagement party."

"Wasn't that just last weekend?"

"I know, but Manny is marvelous." Calen would be proud of her alliteration. "He dropped by my studio yesterday." She put her hand over Nina's wrist. "He actually asked Sheridan where he could find me. Can you believe he sought me out like that?"

Nina tilted her head. "He sounds amazing, but what happened to the other guy?"

"Charles? Oh, that didn't work out. Seems he can't handle dating a woman who has sporadic anxiety attacks."

This time Nina put her hand over Emma's and frowned. "I'm so sorry. He sounds like a jerk."

The thought of him still stung a bit, and she'd only watched half a day's worth of Mr. Bean this time. So maybe that meant she'd been more in love with the idea of Charles and not Charles himself? He'd certainly shown his true colors.

Or maybe she just wanted to live the dream, like Sheridan was. Met Prince Charming, fell in love, nearly lost him, and now was about to live her happily ever after with a magical wedding in a few months.

Swooooooooon…sigh…just like the movies…

"It's fine. I'm fine." She waved her hand at Nina as she looked away. No need to let her see the waterworks threatening in her eyes. At some point, she had to learn how to pick the right guy, one who didn't think of her panic attacks as a defect. She'd certainly had enough practice looking. And she had it on good authority that her heart had put in a transfer request if it happened again.

Manny had to be the one. Had to be.

Chapter Three

What will it be like dining at a restaurant with a chef?

She hadn't thought about it until they walked into the restaurant. Will Manny critique the food the entire time, the way Calen critiqued package descriptions in the grocery store? Of course, he only did that to make her laugh.

But this place seemed more upscale than Madilyn's. Clean lines and lots of windows brought the view of the Gulf inside as part of the setting. Very mid-century modern in its design.

The hostess led them to a booth that overlooked a walkway leading to the dock. A profusion of plants filled oversized planters situated in the middle of the decking below. The entire scene made her inhale deeply and then exhale. A layer of her stressful week sloughed off like a bad sunburn.

"Great view." She tore her gaze from the incredible scenery to look at Manny.

"I agree." The twinkle in his eyes told her he meant her.

He reached across the table and held her hand. "I'm glad you like it. I love this place."

He kept smiling at her too, with his big, bright white smile. Was this how Kate Bosworth's character felt in *Win a Date with Tad Hamilton*? Manny certainly gave Josh Duhamel a run for his money. She'd gladly play Rosalee to his Tad any day.

"You have an amazing smile." The words flooded out in a gush of emotion before she could stop herself.

"Thank you. So do you." He released her hand to touch her face. "I love your freckles."

Emma did a sharp intake and felt her cheeks grow warm. She hadn't been out in the sun enough today to get burned, so it was all him. None of her past relationships had started out this smoothly. Was Manny as enamored with her as she was with him?

Calin's voice sounded in her head again. *Breathe, Emma.*

She smiled to mask her inhale, then exhaled just as their server came to the table. Manny asked several questions about the specials, which gave her a few minutes to recompose herself. If she didn't pace herself, she'd pass out before they finished their meal and blow her chances with him.

Manny settled back into his side of the booth with one arm stretched out on the back of the seat. "So, Emma...tell me more about yourself."

She loved the way her name rolled off his lips, the way the 'a' lingered on his tongue, giving just a hint of his bilingual heritage. And the brief pause he allowed before his next word; as if he were savoring the sound of her name.

"Well, I paint." She let out a nervous laugh. "But you already know that. I teach classes part-time at the local art college and privately as well."

He leaned forward. "Private lessons?"

"Yes, small classes. The project I was working on yesterday is for one of those."

"What other kinds of art do you teach?"

"Mostly fine art classes at the college. Privately, it varies. Landscape painting, figure drawing—"

"Figure drawing? You mean like nudes? You must use models, right?"

"Sometimes, or my students take turns drawing each other if I can't find a model. Uh, with their clothes on, that is." Another nervous laugh. She swallowed. "I didn't want you to think anything weird was going on."

He leaned forward as he brought her hand to his lips and kissed her fingers just below her knuckle line. "I've never posed for an artist. Sounds like…fun."

Her heart hit the floor, bounced, and stuck to the ceiling like a wet noodle. The man made her weak in the knees. Good thing they were sitting. "Well, that would certainly be interesting."

"I'm serious. I'd be happy to be your model." He smiled. "And with clothes on."

Did she just burst into flames? Or had management turned off the air conditioning?

She picked up her menu and fanned herself. "Our server keeps looking over to see if we're ready to order."

"Oh, right." He let go of her hand and picked up his menu.

Emma hadn't actually seen their server looking, but she imagined that was the case. Manny certainly knew how to match her intensity. So unexpected…

She scanned down the menu and picked the first dish that jumped out at her, then peeked over the top to study Manny's face again. His expression had turned serious as he studied the selection. Dark brows dipped into a V-shape above the most beautifully shaped nose she'd ever seen on a man. His well-defined lips pursed against the finger he held against his mouth in thought. And then his jaw. Though a tad cliché, sculpted fit the bill. Her mind became a canvas as she imagined how she'd paint him.

He glanced up and smiled when he caught her staring at him and then quirked one brow up as if to tease her. He certainly knew how to flirt with the best of them. What did a guy like him see in a girl like her, anyway?

He was definitely model material, and she definitely was not.

Calen moved the container in slow circles under the steamer wand to maximize the froth. Chai tea latte with extra cardamom. Not cinnamon. Kaleena's standing order. Since the coffee shop tended to be slow until after the early dinner crowd turned into dessert and coffee foot traffic, he'd decided to make Kaleena's order early and bring it over to her himself.

Something he did occasionally, but on this one, he had an agenda. He needed some wisdom. And the 4-1-1 on Manny.

After dusting the top with cardamon, he snapped a cover on the disposable coffee cup. He waved Steph over to take over the counter. "Be right back."

"Sure thing." She took her station behind the register as if ready for someone to magically appear in front of her. Couldn't fault her for her determination. And since he'd hired her three months ago, Steph had turned into his most reliable employee.

Crossing Pineapple Avenue between crosswalks this time

of day wasn't hard. But he did do his due diligence to make sure there weren't any retired snowbirds backing out of the parking spaces. The narrow street sometimes threw them for a loop.

When he walked into Sass & Sun Fashions, he did a quick inventory of the store. Empty at the moment. Maybe Kay would have time for a chat after all....

She looked up from the register. "Well, hey there, neighbor."

He held her cup up. "Shop was slow, so I thought I'd bring it over for you."

"You are a Godsend, Calen Cooper." She picked up her drink, inhaled, and sighed.

"Rough day?"

She took a sip and *mmmed*. "Not anymore."

He gave a small bow. "Glad to be of service."

"Much appreciated." She picked up a couple of items and walked over to one of her shelves. "Something on your mind?"

"What makes you ask?"

She turned around and pointed at him. "That expression. Usually means you're chewing on something. So cough it up." She snorted at her own pun.

He tried not to moan. And failed. "That the best you can do?"

"Considering the day I've had? Yes. So get to it."

He gave a sheepish glance toward her dressing rooms. "This one may require some ottoman time."

She broke into a full grin. "I'll put up my sign."

Calen made his way to the back area as Kay put her 'closed for 15 minutes' sign up and locked the door.

The oversized olive green ottoman in the middle of the changing room area had a bit of a reputation on Pineapple

Avenue. First, because the previous shop owner died on it, which Kay didn't find out until she bought the space, and then had it thoroughly cleaned. Now the changing area not only served her customers but also the occasional business neighbor in need of advice.

Kaleena Brooks was a whiz at advice.

And sometimes a little insider information, which was what he needed today.

He dropped onto the soft velvet cushion and leaned his forearms on his knees.

Kay sat down next to him. "Ok, spill it."

"Man, you are full of bad metaphors today."

She arched a finely drawn brow at him. "Says the beggar who's being choosey with his fifteen minutes."

He ran his hands through his hair before standing up. "It's about Emma."

Kay shot him a side-long glance. "What about her?"

"More specifically, it's about Manny. She's dating him."

"Sheridan mentioned something about that."

Calen rushed to sit back down next to Kay. "What do you know about him?"

She shrugged. "Not much, really. Sheridan did mention he can be a player at times but thinks highly of him. And he's always very polite when I come in to pick up my orders. Seems like an all-around nice guy."

"So, he dates a lot of women?"

She barked a laugh. "Honey, you'd have to ask him that." She patted his knee. "Why are you so concerned? Is something going on between you and Emma?"

"No. Not at all. She's my best friend, and I'm trying to look out for her."

"Like you did at Sheridan's engagement party?"

He stood, rubbing the back of his neck. "That was just a

misunderstanding. I apologized to both of them. Emma understands I was trying to protect her."

Kay turned her head and narrowed her right eye in question. "Are you sure that's all it was?"

"Of course. What else would it be?" First Mav, now Kay? Why all of a sudden did his friendship with Emma seem under examination?

She raised her brows at him. "You tell me."

He shook his head. "Nothing to tell. We've been friends for years. I just want to make sure she doesn't get her heart wrecked again."

"Again?"

"Yeah, she falls fast and then hard when the guy dumps her." Or she dumps him because he can't deal with her panic attacks.

"Oh, I'm sorry to hear that. She's blessed to have a friend like you in her life. Maybe she just needs some help to understand what kind of guy is right for her."

Why was Kay studying him like that? Seriously? "Yeah, maybe…"

She did a little hop as she shifted on the ottoman. Excitement lit up her eyes. "Let me ask you this. What if Manny turns out to be the one?"

Now there was a question he hadn't expected. "The one…"

"You know. *The One*. Will you be okay with not being the only man in her life?"

Yeah, he knew what she meant, but he hadn't really considered that angle. "Of course. She's had boyfriends in the past, and they seemed fine with our friendship."

"But has she had any long-term relationships?"

He paused. "Nothing longer than a few weeks. She seems to have a type. And I have my theories on that."

"Which are?"

Should he share something that personal about Emma?

"Calen, you know I would never share anything you tell me in confidence, but I also don't want you to feel pressured to tell me something that's none of my business."

He ran a hand over his mouth. "Emma's parents divorced just before we became friends in middle school. By high school, her mother had remarried and Emma considered her stepfather her dad. But sometimes she still struggled with it, especially on her birthday."

"Did her father not keep in contact?"

"He tried at first, then just stopped calling. Sometimes she would imagine he was a CIA agent and had to *go dark* to protect his family." He did air quotes for emphasis.

Kay made a *tsking* sound. "Poor kid. That kind of rejection can steer a person's life."

Calen nodded. "When she showed me a picture of him a few years back, the pieces fell in place."

"The guys she dates are like him?"

"Yep, tall, dark, and never stick around."

"So she's seeking her father's acceptance over and over again. Have you ever brought this up to her?"

"No, I'm not sure how, to be honest. It's a touchy subject."

Kay pushed herself up and patted him on the shoulder. "Like I said, she's blessed to have a friend like you in her life."

"I suppose."

"I'm going to keep that sweet girl in my prayers." Kay pointed at him. "And sometimes people don't realize what—or who—they need most is standing right in front of them."

Chapter Four

Emma unlocked the door to her studio. "I prefer coming here in the evening when it's quiet."

Manny flashed another brilliant smile at her. "I can imagine. I do that sometimes at Madilyn's, especially if I'm trying to fine-tune a recipe."

She dropped her keys into her purse and dropped it on the floor by her desk. "When is that place quiet?"

"Early in the morning. Then I can have the kitchen to myself."

"Can't you do that at home?"

He laughed and linked his fingers with hers. "Do you like to paint at your apartment?"

"No way. Not enough space to spread out. And then I have to clean it all up and put everything away."

"Exactly."

Again, she felt overwhelmed by how connected she and Manny seemed to be. A sudden thought hit her. "You're an artist with food."

He tugged her to him and brushed back the tendrils of

hair dangling down one side of her face. "I love that you think I'm an artist."

The scent of him—a mixture of soap, a subtle cologne, and maybe something else—tantalized her senses. He was so close. And getting closer.

Her heart sped and her breath caught as he leaned toward her. Their first kiss was about to happen. She had to remember every moment and catalog it in her mind. Good thing she got rid of the Charles files to make room. She'd need the extra space for this one.

She tilted her face up as his lips caught hers. His arms slid around her, drawing her against him. The warmth of his hands on her back spread through her blouse to her skin. She could lose herself right here and never come back to reality.

Emma slid her hands around his neck and wove her fingers into the back of his thick, coarse hair.

Manny tightened his arms around her at first and then pulled back. Desire darkened his eyes, which she found interesting, since she didn't think they could get any darker.

"I don't want to move too fast. I hope you're okay with that."

Until air filled her lungs again, she could only nod at first. She croaked an answer. "Perfectly okay."

He dropped his hands to his sides. "How about I pose for you? I want to see you in action."

She held the edge of her desk to steady herself. How did his words disarm her so much, let alone his kiss? "I...I'd love to." She scampered to get the barstool she used for models and placed it in the middle of the room. "Sit in whatever pose you'd like."

She caught another whiff of his scent as he sat down and resisted the urge to initiate another kiss.

Manny sat on the stool with one foot on the lower bar and the other on the floor. Then he leaned on his raised knee. "How's this?"

Was he kidding? The man looked like he just stepped out of a magazine. "Perfect."

Why did she keep using that word? If Calen were here, he'd say something like, "Is that your word of the day?" And then give her that funny little smirk that happened when he raised one side of his mouth in a sarcastic smile.

She vowed to do better as she set up her easel. "Just about ready." Once she had her oversized sketch pad in place, she pulled her hair into a bun and stuck two drawing pencils into it while she searched for a blending stick.

"Do you always do that?"

She glanced up from the open drawer she stood over. "Do what?"

"Stick your paintbrushes and pencils into your hair."

Her cheeks warmed as she dropped her gaze back to the contents of her tool drawer. Why should she feel embarrassed? "Yeah, that way I always know where they are."

"I see."

Now he probably thought she was weird. "I tend to lose them otherwise. My way of staying organized, I guess."

His smile darkened his eyes as he looked at her again like he had before their kiss. The man had sex appeal on demand, like she had Mr. Bean episodes on YouTube. "I think it's adorable."

Adorable? No one had ever called her that. Sometimes Calen called her *adorkable* when she did dorky artist stuff. What Calen called *artsy*.

But no one had ever told her she was adorable.

She swallowed and went to work, capturing Manny's overall physique first in a light sketch to capture the mood of the pose and his proportions. "Are you doing okay? Still comfortable?"

"I'm good."

Good was an understatement. The man was...*perfect*. She really needed to expand her vocabulary.

She swapped pencils for a harder lead and added detail to his shirt—the way it fell open at the collar and revealed the curve of his collarbone into what she imagined was a muscular shoulder and...chest.

"What part are you drawing right now?"

She stopped and met his sultry gaze. "Um, the collar of your shirt and your neck area."

And chest. Just say it.

He lifted his hands to the top button of his shirt. "Should I take it off?"

"No!" She'd combust on sight if he did that. "I mean, that's okay. I like the dimension your shirt adds. It's linen, right?" Now she was resorting to small talk to hide her intense attraction. He had to know the effect he had on her, yet he wanted to take things slowly. The man was an enigma.

"Yeah. Keeps me cool in the heat."

She stood up straight and stared at him. Cool was also not a word she would associate with Manny. At all. Nor herself at the moment. Had she left the thermostat turned up? She sketched the rest of his shoulders, torso, and arms. Now his hands, but she needed a closer look.

The artist in her took over and pushed her away from the protection of her easel. "I need to see your hands up close for a minute. Helps me get the structure and proportions."

He held his hands out.

"Could you put them back where you had them?"

"Sure." He draped one over his leg and leaned the other on the stool again. "How's this?"

"Perfect." She nearly did an eye roll at herself. Seriously. She'd download a dictionary app on her phone and start studying. Calen would be so proud.

After she studied his draped hand, she moved her inspection to his other one. The pressure of his weight added an interesting dimension to the muscle structure on the top of his hand and into his wrist. As she straightened to go back to her easel, Manny caught her wrist and pulled her back.

"My turn to study your hands."

Her nervous laugh made a reappearance. "They're just ordinary hands."

"I sincerely doubt that." He took the pencil from her hand and pushed it into her bun. Then he kissed her palm. "These are hands that make the world a more beautiful place."

Could she swoon and kiss the man silly for the rest of her life? Because if he kept talking to her like that, she'd wind up proposing first.

Breathe, Emma.

She entwined her fingers with his. "And what about you? Don't you make the world a better place by preparing exquisite dishes that delight the senses? Sounds like art to me."

His smile slipped for a moment. Had she touched a nerve somehow? "Did I say something wrong?"

He dropped his gaze as he shook his head. "No, not at all." When he lifted his chin, she had no doubt about Manny's ability to do more than giving her sultry looks. The seriousness of his expression reached into her chest and claimed whatever part of her heart she'd held in check.

She could do nothing but remain a captive to his gaze and wait for him to express what lay deep in his heart.

Yep, total goner.

"I studied under chefs in New York and LA to perfect my art because that's how I see it."

She nodded. "Of course."

"You're the first woman to see that, too. Most just see me as a guy who can cook."

"I would love to see you in action." Her words came out low and husky. She hadn't intended to turn his words back on him. But Manny seemed to have that effect on her.

He stood and drew her to him again. And just as he was about to kiss her, he stopped. "I would love to show you."

———

Once the morning rush died down, Calen untied his apron and tossed it under the counter. He had a mission this morning, and he'd not relent until he succeeded. Namely, convincing his best friend to go after a shot at seeing her incredible artwork in an official gallery showing.

And not just any showing, but one that could launch her career on a national level. Something she'd dreamed about as far back as he could remember. When their high school art club put on a show for the students and parents, Emma had taken charge of creating a true gallery experience with sparkling cider, hors d'oeuvres, and borrowed plants and potted trees from a local nursery.

She'd wanted to create the full experience not only for herself but for her friends, too. Even Calen had taken part by creating a flip book of his best poetry, which Emma displayed on an ornate pedestal that she found in an old junk shop. Didn't matter that she wound up having a meltdown the morning of the show. She'd said it was totally worth it to see everyone's art on display.

He grabbed the forms and scanned the walls of his shop, which displayed several of Emma's pieces. Every couple of months, a customer would buy one—more often during tourist season. He had no doubt that Emma had what it took to be a professional artist. She already was in all truth.

Now if he could convince her of that.

"Hey Steph, take over for me. I need to run an errand."

"Off to see Emma?" Her lilted tone implied she suspected there was something more to his intentions.

He forced down the rush of protest that wanted to blurt out of his mouth, lest the man doth protest too much. Oh, the Shakespearian irony…

"Why do you ask?"

She raised her hands in surrender. "Sorry. I thought she was your girlfriend."

Guess he didn't shove his resentment down enough. "Nope, just my best friend. Since middle school."

"That's cool." She avoided looking at him.

"What?" Why did he care what she thought, anyway? He had better things to do today than worry about someone else's opinion of his relationship with Emma.

Steph shrugged. "I know I haven't been working here that long. Just seems like there's more there."

He probably waited two seconds too long to reply. "And you would be mistaken." He dashed around the counter and headed toward the door. "I'll be right back. Just need to get these signed and submitted."

Afternoon humidity smacked him in the face as he stepped outside. Dark clouds had moved in, signaling the impending afternoon thunderstorm coming their way. He broke into a jog down Pineapple Avenue and crossed over Lemon. The artists' warehouse sat tucked behind one of the largest hotels in downtown Sarasota.

He checked his watch. Unless she had a change of plan, Emma should be in her studio prepping for her evening figure drawing class. He'd convince her to sign the forms and then drop them off at the gallery on his way back to the coffee shop.

Rumbles of thunder sounded in the distance. As he opened the main door to the warehouse, plump drops of rain dotted the sidewalk with a promise of more to come.

The cool air inside hit the moisture on his arms, bringing a rush of goose bumps to the surface. A mishmash of smells indicative of various art media Calen associated with the creative world of the artist's warehouse filled his nose. Much like he linked the smell of an old bookstore to writing.

Emma's studio door stood open.

He sauntered in, careful to keep the paperwork behind his back.

She fought with a mangled mess of an easel in the middle of the studio space. Several others already stood in a circle with adjacent stools. A chaise lounge, a small ottoman, and several other items sat in the middle, ready for a model.

He put the papers down on her desk and quickened his step. "Here, let me help you with that."

She handed over the distorted metal. "Thanks. Not sure that one's salvageable, though. It got crushed the other night."

"How'd that happen?" He tried to straighten one of the legs.

"Oh, nothing major, really." She shrugged. "I was sketching Manny, and we may have gotten a little…silly."

Calen stared at her, unsure of what to say.

"No, not that." She swatted at him as she blushed. "Manny was trying to teach me to do the samba. Turns out he's an amazing dancer too."

Sketched Manny? Calen tried to recall the last time she'd sketched him. Probably years.

"Wow, guess you really like this guy." He'd only danced with Emma once and that was years ago at a high school dance. And only by default because her date dumped her in the middle of a song. They spent the rest of the evening on her couch watching Mr. Bean and eating popcorn as he passed her tissues.

Her face broke into a smile that replaced the sunshine missing because of the storm outside. Figuratively speaking, that is. But just the same…he'd seen Emma through many a crush, but this one seemed more serious. And moving faster than the norm…how much longer would it last before they spent a day on her couch watching Mr. Bean again?

"I do, Calen. He's…perfect."

If their dialogue were on a page, there would definitely be exclamation points to reflect his internal reaction. "That's a strong word, Emma."

"I know, but it's the perfect word." She covered her heart with her hands and laughed in a giddy manner. "I know. I'm being redundant."

Something about this made his stomach clench. Emma was falling harder than usual for this guy. "Things seem to be moving fast, don't you think?"

She sat down on the lounger. "Manny said the same thing last night. He wants to take things slow. Take our time to get to know each other."

"Really, now."

"Don't be sarcastic. I can tell he means it. I don't think I've ever met anyone like him before." She stared at the rain streaming down the windows. "Something's different this time, Calen. I can feel it."

And he could see it in her eyes when she faced him. The tightness in his stomach traveled to his chest. He wanted to caution her, tell her to be careful with her heart. Because this crush could do some serious damage, but he'd keep his concerns to himself for now.

"Hey, I have something for you." He walked back to her desk to get the gallery paperwork. That's when he noticed her sketch pad. Manny's image covered most of the large sheet. Emma had captured his form, unlike anything he'd seen before. The detail and life she'd portrayed with a simple pencil sketch—astounding.

He wanted to rip it to shreds.

Calen took a deep breath and returned to where Emma still sat. "I've filled them out for you. All you have to do is sign the agreement."

She frowned as she took the papers. "What exactly am I agreeing to?"

"The art show. They want six finished pieces by the end of next month."

She gasped. "Six? Calen, I don't know, that's a lot. I'm not sure I'm up to this."

He could tell if he didn't downplay things some, she would head into a panic attack. "Are you kidding? You already have several finished pieces hanging in my shop. You could work on one and just pick the rest from your completed works."

She held a hand to her chest as she paced and breathed. "I know, but those aren't gallery quality."

"You gave me junk for my shop?"

She stopped and laughed, which was his intention. "No, I mean they're older work. I feel like something has shifted and the quality of my work has improved. I'd want to do brand new pieces for something like this."

Shifting her focus to her work always seemed to settle her, but he wasn't ready to let it go. "You can do this, Emma. I know you can. That sketch you did of Manny is amazing."

He wanted to take the words back, but as much as he hated saying it, the truth was more important than his opinion of the guy. He'd keep that to himself for now.

"And I'll help you get ready. Whatever you need. Your classes at the college are finished for the summer, so you'll have more time. I can even help you with your private classes. Just tell me what to do."

She tapped her lips with her finger, which, for some reason, brought an acute awareness to her lips. The upsweep of the corners made her appear as if she smiled all the time. The perfect—he'd have to work on that one too—proportion of her bottom lip to her upper one, like the soft folds of gardenia petals overlapping. He wanted to whip out his notepad and write a sonnet about her mouth. What was wrong with him?

He dropped his gaze to the papers he held out. "Come on, Emma. Sign the agreement. The gallery owner arranging the show didn't even need a portfolio submission. He saw your pieces in my shop—the ones you think are subpar—and said all you had to do was sign the agreement."

That mischievous gleam in her eyes spiked again. She jumped up from the lounge. "I'll sign if you agree to a double date."

"What?" Where did that come from?

"I want to go on a double date with my best friend."

"But I'm not dating anyone at the moment."

"I know. I have someone in mind."

"Oh, so you mean a blind date?"

"Yep." She did a mock clap with her hands. "It'll be fun! And Nina is great. You will *looove* her."

Love was a really strong word, and one he didn't easily use. "I don't know."

She grabbed a pen from her desk and held it up. "Do you want me to sign the papers or not?"

He should get the friend-of-the-year-award for this one. "Fine."

She took the documents, signed, and then held them out to him. "We are going to have a blast."

A smile lingered on her lips. Judging by her distant expression, she'd already left the present and was planning his dating demise. Or her next painting. Didn't matter. He'd managed to help her avoid a panic attack and got her to agree to the art show.

The tightness in his chest lifted and something akin to pleasure took its place. He loved seeing Emma inspired. And this was her time to shine. He'd make sure of it.

Even if it meant going on a blind date with Emma and Manny.

Chapter Five

A humid ocean breeze teased the hair dangling around her face as a gorgeous red-orange sun made its slow descent toward a blue-green ocean. Waves lapped gently onto the shore, where seagulls and skimmers took turns hunting for small fish.

The sky shifted from golden yellows and pinks to a blush of rose and warm purples...God creating a master-piece in the sky and her favorite time of the day on the beach...

Emma tugged on Manny's arm to come to a stop. "Wait for it."

"The sunset?"

"No, if you watch the sun as it dips below the horizon, sometimes you'll see a momentary burst of green."

"Really? You're not just making that up now, are you?" The collar of his white linen shirt blew up against his neck.

"I promise it's worth the wait." She laid her head against his shoulder as they watched the sun finish its descent.

A burst of green light flashed as the top of the sun disappeared.

Manny chuckled. "That's amazing."

"It's caused by the refraction of sunlight."

His gaze dropped to her lips, and his voice deepened with his whisper. "Not only creative but smart too."

She lifted her chin as he lowered his head to kiss her. He brought his hand up to cup her face as he lingered, tender but not demanding. Manny made her feel…well, loved. She wanted to tell him she was falling in love with him almost from day one, but she'd controlled herself and allowed the relationship to progress without giving it a shove.

And they'd spent time together almost every day. Any day they weren't together, they spent on the phone talking, sometimes for hours. And texting in-between.

Was he falling for her as hard as she was for him? He seemed pretty taken with her. As much time as they'd spent together, she couldn't imagine him dating anyone else.

"What's going through that beautiful mind of yours?" He tapped the tip of her nose.

Emma tilted her head back. "You don't want to know."

He tugged her back when she tried to resume their walk. "But I do, Emma. Seriously, I mean it."

The fading light created a glow around his head from behind. Should she take the risk and be honest or keep her concerns to herself? They hadn't dated that long. "I was thinking about how much time we spend together."

His brows dipped down in that cute way when he was concerned. "We've been together almost every day, haven't we?"

"Yes, we have."

"Has it been too much for you?"

"No, not at all. I just…" This was harder than she

thought. Would she go home dreamy, like she had almost every night this week? Or destroyed and desperate for a Mr. Bean binge-fest again?

"Just what?"

"I was just wondering if you were dating someone else; if you even had time to." She gave a nervous laugh but kept her chin tucked, unwilling to let him see her that vulnerable.

He tipped her head up with his finger. "The answer is no. And I don't want to."

She met his gaze and found herself lost in his sincerity.

Then his expression shifted and doubt simmered in the depths of his dark eyes. "Do you? Want to see other people?"

"No!" She took a breath. "No, I don't."

His smile marked the return of his usual confidence. "Then good. We are officially exclusive. I like the sound of that."

"Me too." She loved the way he always held her hand whenever they were together. The way he'd link his fingers into hers, which usually led to him drawing her in for a kiss.

Before they left the shore, Manny leaned over and grabbed something from the damp sand. He held his hand out to her, revealing a small, white sand dollar about the size of a quarter.

She brushed more of the sand away. "It's so cute. And complete."

He held up her hand and placed it in the middle of her palm. "It's for you."

"But you found it."

"I want you to have it, Emma. As a reminder of tonight."

She smiled as she ran a finger over the top of the delicate skeleton. "Did you know that if you break it open, there are these little dove-shaped pieces inside the middle? They're a symbol of peace, too."

He chuckled. "No. There you go, being beautiful and brilliant again. That makes it even more special."

Beautiful and brilliant? And he wanted to be exclusive? Had she stepped into a dream or onto the set of a romance movie? She cradled his gift in her hand. As soon as she got home, she'd put it in her memory box.

She ran her hand down his forearm and linked fingers with his. "Have you always lived in Sarasota?"

"No. I was born in Miami but went to culinary school in New York. Worked there for a while before moving to LA."

"Wow. New York *and* LA. What made you want to settle for Sarasota?"

"Settle? I don't see it that way at all." He scanned the fading horizon and held his free hand out. "We live in paradise, in case you didn't notice."

"That is true. I guess since I grew up here and haven't really been anywhere else, it seems boring compared to New York and LA."

He dipped his head as he shrugged. "I admit, I miss the big city vibe sometimes, but this place feels like home. And I get to be a sous chef at an amazing downtown restaurant."

"Do you think you'll ever go back?"

"Maybe. But right now, I just want to think about us."

They'd reached his car. Manny kissed the back of her hand. "I can't seem to stop kissing you."

"Do you hear me complaining?"

Either what she said or the way she said it must have sparked something in him. He dropped her hand and pulled her into a kiss that demanded a response from her; as if to seal their declaration of exclusivity. And she answered with all she had until he pulled back and just held her.

"I don't think I've ever felt like this before, Emma."

She wrapped her arms around his waist and laid her head against his chest. His heart thumped under her ear as fast as hers did. Something about his words thrilled and concerned her all at once. Perhaps it was the tinge of hesitancy she detected in his voice. Did he regret their decision to be exclusive?

Or was he afraid of what he was feeling for her?

In the full light of day, would he take a sudden dash for singleness again?

Calen checked his watch again to confirm she was now thirty minutes late. Tonight was their weekly movie night but no Emma. She must have had another date and forgotten to tell him. Which she'd never done before. Until Manny…

Yep, time would now be defined as before and after Manny. Calen kicked himself for not listening to the inkling he had before heading over to text her first.

So why was he still sitting on her stoop and not going home? He pushed his hands through his hair as he lowered his head. Emma's myriad of boyfriends had never bothered him before. So why now? What threat did he perceive in the cosmos of their friendship?

Maybe going on a blind date would be good for him after all. He'd become quite comfortable with the status quo of his and Emma's friendship. Perhaps too comfortable…

"Calen, what are you doing here?"

He jerked his head up so fast that pain shot up one side of his neck, making him cringe. "Movie night, remember?"

She gasped, then covered her mouth. "I'm so sorry! I

totally forgot." She sat down on the step next to him, letting her bag slide down next to her feet. "Manny surprised me with a picnic dinner on the beach."

Powdery white sand still nestled in the corners of her pink polished toes, and she smelled like coconuts.

"We can do it another time." He pushed up from the step, then grunted and fell back. The muscle in his neck went into overdrive, shooting pain down into his shoulder.

"Calen, are you okay?" She hovered over him, her expression concerned.

"Yeah, I think I pulled a muscle." He rubbed the side of his neck.

"Here, let me see if I can help with that." She got on her knees behind him and started massaging his neck and shoulder. "Wow, you have quite the knot there."

She pushed harder, making him grunt again, but the muscle released as the warmth of her hands seeped into his skin, making him relax. He closed his eyes. "That's better."

Her hands traveled up his neck as she continued to massage upward. "Hey, your hair is almost long enough."

Her fingers combing through the front of his hair sent an odd sensation through him. Comfort at first, but then something shifted, making him aware of a longing he'd broken an acquaintance with a long time ago.

He let his head tip back with her hands. When he opened his eyes, he locked gazes with Emma's crystal blues. She stopped moving and stared back at him. Her lips captured his attention and for a split second, he imagined what it would be like to kiss her.

Calen jerked his head up, sending his neck muscle into a spasm again, but he ignored it. "It's getting late. I should go."

Emma picked up her bag in an awkward fashion. "We'll reschedule, okay?"

"Sure. No problem." Right now, he needed to get out of here. Fast. But then he remembered he'd brought the hanger he'd had made for her bird feeder. He pulled it out of the sack he'd brought and held it out to her. "I asked Mav to make this for your bird feeder."

Her mouth formed a small circle before breaking into pure joy. "Calen! I love it." She giggled. "I've been reminding myself to breathe a lot these days."

Her eye roll and tone implied her complete infatuation with Manny.

Probably a good thing they weren't doing a movie tonight. He didn't think he could handle any more Manny-talk.

"I'm glad you love it. Good night, Emma." He'd almost reached the sidewalk when she called him back. He did a slow turn, grateful for the cover of the impending night because the last thing he needed was for her to see on his face what was racing through his mind. "Yeah?"

She left the step and walked toward him. "I know we had a deal about that blind date thing, but if you don't want to do it, that's okay."

He tucked his chin so his hair would partially hide his face. "You'll still do the art show?"

She exhaled her resignation. "Of course. I'd be crazy not to, right?"

"Right."

"So, no double date?" She had that look on her face that meant she wanted the opposite of what she was asking.

He wanted to say no, should just say no and be done with it. But in truth, he needed to get Emma out of his head. "Set up the date. Sounds fun."

She did a double clap with her hands before running up and hugging him. "Thank you! It'll be great. You'll see. I'll plan the whole thing."

He let himself hug her back like he always did, but something felt different this time, less comforting and more intoxicating. The way she felt in his arms and her scent. He had a sudden urge to nuzzle her neck. He didn't want to let her go.

What was wrong with him?

Why, after all these years, would he find himself drawn to her in that way again?

She stepped back, smiled, and headed to her apartment.

His arms felt empty. He studied her for a moment. "Why now?"

She turned around, tugging her bag onto her shoulder. "What do you mean?"

"This is the first time you've wanted to do the double date thing. Why now?"

The warmth of the sun couldn't hold ground with the smile she gave him. "Manny and I are so happy together. I want you to have that too, Calen."

He nodded, then waved good night. Once inside his car, he stared at her door. His heart still raced and the image of her looking down at him filled his mind every time he closed his eyes. Those piercing blue eyes could drown a person in love if they were so lucky to be the object of her affection.

And the way she felt when he held her…

He shook his head and started the engine. A blind date was just what he needed to clear his head and move back into the friend zone.

Chapter Six

After picking Manny's brain for suggestions, Emma found something a little different and fun. She'd overheard two of her students in one of her private classes talking about a sushi place downtown. Sounded like a great place for interesting conversation, at the very least about the food if nothing else gelled over the evening.

Nina had agreed to the date without even a bribe or a twist of the arm. And when Emma asked why, Nina simply said she'd heard enough about Calen from her. That he sounded like a great guy.

Did she talk about Calen that much?

Manny had picked her up instead of meeting her in front of the restaurant like she'd told Calen and Nina to do. Guess that was part of their growing girlfriend/boyfriend relationship. She'd spent part of her night doing an inventory of her past relationships, just to compare and assess where she might be in this current relationship. None of them had stayed this good this long.

She'd slept like a baby after that.

As they stood outside waiting, Manny linked his pinky with hers. "Relax. Even if Calen and Nina don't hit it off, we can still have a fun evening, right?"

She shrugged one shoulder. "I suppose."

"It'll be fine." He kissed the tip of her nose, then glanced over her shoulder. "Hey, is that them?"

Emma turned around and looked down the sidewalk. Calen and Nina headed their way, already conversing as if they knew each other.

Nina's laughter reached them as they closed the distance. As did Calen's.

Did they already know each other?

Emma gave them each a hug. "I didn't think you two knew each other."

Calen's lopsided grin appeared as he met Nina's amused expression; as if they already had some kind of secret. "We don't. We both parked in the back and headed in the same direction. So I asked if she was your friend."

"And I said yes." Nina giggled as she widened her eyes. "Turns out we share a love for Shakespeare."

Emma noted the easiness between them. She'd had a feeling they'd hit it off. Just not this fast. "Wow, I'm impressed. I thought Calen was the only one."

"Hey now." His grin belied his protest.

She gave him a playful poke in the side.

Calen mouthed a 'thank you' to Emma when Nina turned to Manny and introduced herself.

Guess she didn't have to worry about how the evening would play out. She couldn't have orchestrated a better first encounter, but something about it seemed to bother her. Maybe she was just tired and hungry. She spent most of her day in the studio working on a piece for the art show. And trying not to panic about how much work she still had to do in such a short amount of time.

Manny opened the door to the restaurant. "Shall we?"

Her first impression of the place did not disappoint. Elegant, cozy, and authentic...the greeter sat them in an isolated part of the restaurant, separated from the rest of the seating area. She couldn't have asked for a more perfect spot.

Manny pulled out a chair for her as did Calen for Nina, which wound up putting the guys across from each other. Emma did an eye check with Calen to make sure he was okay with the arrangement. After all, his and Manny's last encounter in a restaurant resulted in a fistfight.

Calen winked at her. "Great place, Emma."

Nina nodded her agreement. "I've been wanting to check this place out."

Emma beamed. "I know, right? And such a great table too."

"Well, I may have had some influence there." Manny opened his menu.

"What do you mean?" Emma pushed his menu down. "I made the reservation."

"I know, but I called and asked for special seating." Manny shrugged. "I know the chef."

"Of course you do." Emma tried to laugh it off, but couldn't help but feel a tad upstaged. Manny had taken her out to some really magnificent spots over the last few weeks, so her plan had been to impress him for a change.

He reached over and squeezed her hand. "You picked a perfectly good spot."

Why was Manny talking down to her? He'd never done that before. But there'd never been more than just the two of them on their dates so far.

"And the selection is amazing." Nina glanced over the top of her menu.

Manny blasted his smile of a thousand suns at her. "It is. The chef here is one of the best in town."

Emma lowered her menu. "From what I read in the reviews, the Monkey Brain is amazing."

"What kind of place is this?" Calen dropped his menu.

Emma's giggle turned into a full belly laugh that left her unable to speak. She'd waited all day to pull that one on him.

Nina pointed to the appetizer section. "Relax. She's just jerking you around. It's avocado, tuna, and…stuff."

Calen shook his head. "Always the prankster, that one."

"Admit it, you almost bought it." Emma tapped his shin with the tip of her shoe.

Their server arrived with a tray of water glasses, which she placed on the table in front of them as she explained the menu and specials.

Emma couldn't help but notice how the server kept her eyes—and smile—directed at Manny as she spoke. He either didn't mind or was oblivious.

Nina laid her menu down. "I can't decide what to order."

"Are you willing to trust me?" Manny's tone bordered on flirtatious.

Nina bounced her gaze in Emma's direction before replying. "Um, sure?"

Calen's expression looked as if he found out the Monkey Brains were real.

She needed to step in and explain before Nina and Calen bailed on her. "Manny's really great at helping me figure out what I'll enjoy the most."

Nina's uncertainty turned into surprise. "Oh, then, in that case, I'm game."

Manny asked her a series of questions, which Emma knew was to help him figure out what she preferred. But Calen did not look happy. At all. Thankfully, Nina and Manny were too engaged to notice.

Emma kicked his shin hard this time, which made him jump in his seat.

Nina touched his arm. "Are you okay?"

Calen gave her a tight grin. "I'm peachy."

Nina giggled. "Well good. I'm off to the restroom. Try not to miss me too much."

Manny stood with her. "I'll be right back."

Emma tugged on his fingers. "Where are you going?"

"To the kitchen, of course. I want to say hello to the chef." Manny walked off, leaving Calen and Emma alone.

She angled toward him, leaning over the table. "What's with you?"

"Nothing. Why?" He didn't look at her, just continued to study his menu.

"Don't give me that mock innocence, Calen Cooper. You're acting like a grumpy teenager."

He rolled his head back and then gave her an angry stare. "Fine. I'll straighten up just as soon as you tell your date to quit flirting with mine."

"He wasn't flirting. He likes to help."

"That's what you call it?" Sarcasm dripped from his words.

Emma sat back in her chair. What was the point of arguing with him?

Neither one of them said anything else, but Emma didn't miss the range of emotions playing across Calen's face. He usually did that to process the situation before eventually landing on an apology.

"Remember that song?" He gave her a sheepish glance.

"What song?"

He pointed to the speaker on the ceiling. "You're My Satellite."

She tuned into the melody. "Yeah, that horrible high school dance."

"The night wasn't a complete disaster."

Even then, she got dumped. But Manny would be different. She knew it…felt it. "It's still one I'd like to forget."

"Forget what?" Manny sat down.

"The song that's playing. Calen was reminding me of a rather disappointing time in my life."

"Oh?"

Did she really want to talk about how her high school boyfriend dumped her? "It's from when we were teenagers."

Nina returned to the table and sat down. "Teenagers? Please tell me we're not talking about our students?"

———

Calen wanted to kick himself. He hadn't intended for anyone else to hear. But besides that, why did he let a little nostalgia turn up some long-forgotten dirt? "Emma's boyfriend broke up with her in the middle of the dance."

"Oh, that's horrible." Nina tilted her head at Calen. "You were there?"

"Calen was always there." Emma looked as if the words had surprised her. She gave a nervous laugh. "Best friends since middle school."

"That's sweet. So what did you do?" Nina kept staring at him; as if she were trying to figure him out.

Calen couldn't look away from Emma. That evening never faded in his memories, as it marked the beginning of his high school crush on her and the most excruciating year of his life. Good thing he put it behind him.

"He danced with me." She pointed a finger upward to the source of the tune as it ended. The corners of her mouth lifted as she recalled the memory. "To this song. Sang the lyrics to me too until I stopped crying."

And then he took her home and they binge-watched Mr. Bean. That part he'd kind of forgotten because it blended with the other times he'd done that with Emma after a breakup.

Nina squeezed his hand. "You're a great friend."

Manny tipped Emma's chin to look at him. "I can understand why you like that song. 'Shining like a work of art'—that's you, Emma."

Emma's eyes turned glassy just before she closed them to kiss Manny.

Nina made an *awww* sound. "Aren't they adorable?"

Calen wanted to shove the table out of the way and clock Manny on the jaw again. The guy stole his and Emma's song and turned it into something between them. His anger must have shown because Nina poked him in the side and gave him an 'are you okay?' frown.

He pushed a smile he didn't feel in place and nodded. Fortunately, two servers arrived with several platters of sushi and appetizers, distracting everyone from the love fest. The evening continued on a much lighter note of food consumption and topics based solely on the food and the present.

Four entrees arrived, per Manny's arrangements. Nina flipped over hers and thanked Manny several times. Calen had to admit, the guy knew food. And he even complimented Manny's choices, which he could tell made Emma thrilled. So at least he did something right tonight.

He glanced at his watch. The place had emptied except for them and one other couple, who were about to leave. "I think we closed the place down. I'll get the server to bring our checks."

"No need. I've taken care of it already." Manny smiled at him before lifting Emma's hand to kiss her fingers for what Calen estimated had to be the hundredth time.

Calen pulled out his wallet. "I'm happy to pay for Nina and me."

"Like I said, no need." He rose from the table and tugged Emma along with him.

Nina gave him a shy glance and then slung her purse over her shoulder and followed them.

Great. Emasculated by a man. Something Calen never saw coming. He felt like a teenager again, on a date with his parents.

So awkward.

They parted ways after exchanging the customary 'this was great' and 'let's do it again' niceties.

"I'll walk you to your car." Calen matched his stride to Nina's.

"Thanks."

They walked in silence for a few moments.

Nina held her purse in front of her. "You really like her, don't you?"

Why was she asking him that? "You mean Emma? Yeah, we've been best friends for over fifteen years now."

They'd reached Nina's car. She leaned against the door. "I mean, you're really into her."

He shrugged. "I'll admit I had a crush on her after that dance thing, but I got over it."

"Are you sure about that?" Nina crossed her arms and tilted her head.

Here he stood with a beautiful woman who seemed interested in him and they were talking about Emma?

Again, what was wrong with him?

He stared at Nina and realized he hadn't fully appreciated the way her light brown hair curled around her cute face just above the shoulder. She had a natural confidence about her and was easy to be around.

"Yeah, I'm totally sure." He moved closer, tucking her hair behind her ear as he ran his thumb across her cheek. "I'd much rather talk about you."

And he did. Needed to. Enough Emma talk.

Nina rested her hand on his chest, just above his heart. "I'll be honest, Calen."

Uh oh...had he blown it? Was she going to say she didn't want to date someone who wasn't emotionally available? Because he could prove to her that he was. He just needed an evening out with her that didn't include Manny and Emma.

"That's good, because I like honesty." He let out a soft chuckle and then regretted it. Now he felt awkward again.

Nina moved closer to him. Why was she closing the distance between them if she was about to say thanks but no thanks? "I like you and I'd really like to get to know you better. Think we could start with that?"

Hmmm, he liked this girl. She didn't pull punches. "Yeah, I'd really like that too."

"Good." Her soft kiss on his cheek lingered, giving him enough time to catch the floral scent of her skin and hair. Like night blooming jasmine.

Which reminded him of Emma...he mentally shook himself.

As she stepped back and unlocked her car, Calen opened the door for her.

She slid behind the wheel. "Call me when you're ready. Emma knows how to reach me."

He waited until she drove out of the parking lot to head to his car, whistling a tune. He'd get Nina's number from Emma tomorrow and call Nina for an actual date—even thought about what kind of date as he drove home.

That should prove he didn't have a thing for Emma right there. He wanted to go out with Nina and see where things went. Maybe build a relationship with her. They already had a love for Shakespeare in common. The thought brought about a sense of anticipation for what might develop between them.

Until he realized he'd whistled 'You're My Satellite' the entire drive home.

Chapter Seven

After a busy morning at the coffee shop, Calen had left the front to Steph and ducked into his office to finish the flyer he'd started the night before. The art gallery had loved his idea of catering a special pre-showing with a café theme on the sidewalk.

He'd developed a decent following for Java Jerry's on Facebook over the last several years to connect more with the downtown community. Once he showed the flyer to the gallery owner, he'd create a Facebook event. Emma would love it. She'd see firsthand what the folks on Pineapple Avenue could accomplish for one of their own.

Which reminded him, he needed to ask Kaleena for some ideas for some custom T-shirts for his team to wear for the event. Something that would highlight the gallery's promotion of local artists. They'd even wear them before the show for publicity.

And Noah and Sheridan had offered several café tables from their restaurant, as well as several cases of wine, for the event. Nothing like tapping your best friend's 'best-friend-who's-a-girl' to help.

Yeah, he'd play that one out on Emma. The thought made him chuckle out loud.

"What's so funny?"

Calen jerked in surprise so hard that he deleted one of the images on his flyer design. "Shoot!" Thank goodness for undo.

"Now you know how I felt the other day." Emma giggled in the doorway to his office.

He closed the document down in case she got nosy and spun around in his seat. "What are you doing here?"

"Would you like me to leave?" She put her hands on her hips and batted her eyelashes.

"Of course not. Just rarely see you here this time of day. Don't you have a class to teach?"

"It's summer. I'm down to one class. Whatcha working on that made you laugh?"

He spun his head toward his computer. "Oh, that? Just a promotional thing."

"Well, that sounds vague and slightly boring. Care to come out and talk to your best friend for a few minutes before her boyfriend comes?"

Boyfriend...she'd moved to calling Manny her boyfriend. "Does no one have to work except me?"

She swatted his arm as he approached. "He's having coffee with me before he goes in for the lunch shift."

Of course, he was. He's the perfect boyfriend. That he could see that written all over her face whenever she talked about him, and he couldn't recall any of Emma's relationships going this well after several weeks. Which concerned him even more. How many Mr. Bean episodes would it take to recover from this one?

He followed her out to the counter. "Want another cup of that tea I made you?"

"No, surprise me with something fruity and cold. I walked here from the warehouse and now I'm hot."

"You got it." He went to work on putting together a fruit smoothie with her favorites.

The front door jingled and in walked Manny, dressed in all black except for his chef's jacket, which hung open like that day he showed up at her studio. He walked up to Emma and gave her a full-on kiss on the lips.

"Hey, Manny." Calen turned on the blender as Manny started speaking.

Maybe on purpose. Maybe not.

Manny waited to repeat his words until the blender stopped. "Calen, good to see you, man."

"What can I get you?" He'd just treat him like any customer and move on.

"Just a cup of coffee. Black."

Plain coffee? Calen had expected Manny to order something more special. Like espresso with a lime peel. Or a cappuccino.

He continued to prep their drinks as Manny and Emma wandered over to a table under one of her paintings. Manny seemed fully engaged as he smiled and pointed to various parts of the picture. And Emma seemed to sparkle with excitement, which she did anytime someone showed an interest in her work.

Maybe Kay was right about Manny being *The One*. He seemed really into Emma. And interested in her art. The perfect boyfriend? He didn't know about that, but Manny did seem good for Emma.

The thought made him want to pull out his notebook and write an ode to the fickleness of love.

Wait. Where did that come from? He should be happy for Emma.

He *was* happy for Emma.

Calen carried their drink order to the table as they sat down.

"Thanks, Calen." Emma smiled at him.

Yep, she beamed. Just like the line in that song that hadn't left him alone for days. She really was like a piece of art hanging on a wall of stars.

She pulled her hair up in one hand while she rummaged in her bag with the other one. "I can't find my hair band."

"I've got one." Calen pulled his wallet out and tugged out the hair band he kept stored there, just in case.

Emma wrapped her hair into a messy bun. She must have spent more time in the sun lately because her blonde hair had more highlights. "Was that intended for you? Your hair's almost long enough."

Calen shook his head. "No, I keep it in my wallet in case you need it."

She blinked at him; as if caught off guard, then smiled. Did she just blush? "Wow. Thanks, Calen."

Manny gave him a funny look before taking a sip of his coffee. "Could I get some cream?"

"Too hot?"

"No, slightly bitter."

Calen had ordered that bean specially from a roaster in Seattle. "Sure."

He strode back behind the counter, poured some cream into a small carafe, and then returned to their table.

Emma and Manny held hands and leaned in for another kiss.

Calen set the carafe on the table a little too hard. Some cream splashed onto Manny's black shirt.

He jerked back.

"Whoops. Sorry about that." But he wasn't, in all honesty. Guess it was his day to behave like an immature idiot.

Manny waved him off. "No worries. My jacket will cover it."

After frowning at him, Emma leaned over and dabbed at Manny's shirt with her napkin. "There. All better."

Better indeed. Calen picked up the wadded napkin Emma dropped on the table. "Thanks again for setting me up with Nina. She said you could give me her number if I wanted to call her."

"Oh, yeah. No problem." She grabbed her phone from her purse, then swiped the screen a few times. "On its way."

He felt his phone vibrate in his back pocket. "Thanks."

"You're going to call her?" She had expectation written all over her face.

"Yeah, I thought we could go to the Concert in the Park at Selby this weekend."

Emma bounced in her seat with excitement. "That's great! Manny and I are going with Noah and Sheridan. We'll see you there."

"Great." Calen backed up a step before spinning around to return to the counter.

Maybe he'd suggest something different for them to do when he called Nina.

Selby Gardens was one of her favorite places in Sarasota. Emma loved to bring an easel and her watercolors right around this time of year, when many of the spring blooming plants gave their best performance. But her favorite part was the Mangrove Walkway that led to several small decks, giving a scenic view of Sarasota Bay.

She sighed as she leaned against the railing. Boats dotted the water farther out and the sky had begun its shift into sunset.

"The water is very peaceful today." Manny stood next to her with his arm around her waist.

"I love this place. I can't believe you haven't been here yet." She poked him in the chest.

He shrugged. "Different priorities, I guess. I go see restaurants. And taste."

She laughed at him. "I don't know how you do it and stay…stay in such good shape."

His smile turned sultry. "You like my shape?"

Despite the cooler temperature coming with the sunset and a breeze wafting in from the ocean, her face and neck felt hot. "Yes, you have a very nice shape. I've enjoyed sketching and painting you very much."

"With my shirt on."

"Yes." Wow, did he have a way of disarming her with his flirting.

He tipped her chin up with his finger and brushed her lips with his. "I like your shape too."

Her stomach fluttered when she met his gaze, darkened by desire. Behind him, dusk settled in, streaking the sky with purple and dark blue.

Almost Prussian blue…

"There you are." Sheridan's voice came from the main path. She and Noah walked toward them. "I see you two had the same idea of coming a little early to see the sunset."

Emma didn't trust her legs enough to walk, so she leaned against the railing. "Manny has never been here before. I had to show him the best parts of the gardens."

Noah nodded at Manny, and the two men shook hands and bro-hugged. "Perfect evening for a concert."

Sheridan looped her arm through Noah's. "Have you seen Calen and Nina yet?"

Emma tugged out her phone. "He said he'd text when they got here. He wanted to take Nina out to dinner first."

"Aww, how sweet." Sheridan glanced up at Noah with love eyes.

Did she look like that when she looked at Manny? And if she did, did he notice? So far, all his signals told her he was still super interested in her. Maybe the evening would be so romantic that she'd have the perfect time to tell him she was falling for him.

Her phone chimed. "Calen just texted. They're getting seats for us."

Sheridan walked beside Emma while the guys lagged behind, chatting. "You and Manny sure looked cozy."

Emma put a hand to her cheek. "He makes me breathless. He's like those cliché Latin lover type characters you see in the movies, but let me tell you, there is nothing cliché about that man."

"Wow, you're really falling for him. Have you told him how you feel?"

She shook her head. "No, I'm trying not to move too fast. He wants to take things slow, so…"

Sheridan tilted her head back for a moment. "Ah, I see. Well, considering that it's Manny, that's probably a good sign."

"Why?"

She glanced over her shoulder, as did Emma. The guys stood about twenty feet back, gesturing in conversation.

"Manny's dated quite a few women, but never really built a relationship with any of them. Until you, that is."

Emma's heart felt too big for her chest. Knowing that gave her the courage to tell Manny how fast her feelings for him had grown.

They'd reached the concert platform on the far end of the green and made their way to the other side of the seating area.

As she spotted where Nina and Calen sat, he leaned in closer to Nina, who smiled at whatever he was saying and rested her hand on his arm. He was probably quoting Shakespeare to her. Seemed the perfect setting to do so. If the evening event had been Shakespeare in the Park, the two of them would probably be twitching in their seats, ready for the show to begin.

Wow, look at that. Nina really seemed to be into Calen, too. She ran her fingers into the side of his hair that fell in front of his eyes the most, pushing it back. And the way Calen looked at her when she did it? Surprised at first, and then he kind of settled into it. Kind of like when she did that the other night when she found him waiting for her... when she'd forgotten about her plans with her best friend because she was so distracted with Manny.

What kind of friend did that make her?

She'd felt guilty ever since.

Emma quickened her step and waved. "Hi, guys! Great seats." She plopped into the seat next to Calen. "How was your dinner?"

Manny, Sheridan, and Noah filed into the seats next to her.

Nina looked at Calen first, as if waiting for him to say something, but when he hesitated, she half laughed, half giggled. "We wound up talking so long at my place when Calen came to pick me up we missed our reservation, so I made us dinner."

A shyness came over Calen as he smiled. "Turns out Nina is quite the cook."

Manny leaned in front of Emma. "Oh yeah? What did you make?"

Nina shrugged. "Just threw together a frittata."

"I love making frittatas. What do you like to put in yours?"

Nina listed off the ingredients with Calen's help. Sounded...cozy.

Emma kept finding herself staring at Calen as he interacted with Nina, fascinated to see this side of him. What he was like on a date...

The performers stepped onto the platform set up on the far end of the green. Emma settled back against Manny as he slipped his arm across her shoulders. From the corner of her eye, she noticed Calen do the same thing with Nina. Clearly, they were having a great second date. She should be thrilled, especially since she'd played matchmaker.

The musicians played covers of hit songs ranging from the late nineties to current hits. Most at a slower beat than the original, which gave the music more of a moody feel when accompanied by the throaty vocals of their main singer.

Two different couples stood in quick succession to each other and slow-danced. Next thing she knew, Sheridan and Noah had joined in and Manny was tugging on her to come with him.

She took his hand and followed him to a spot not too far from the platform. Manny rested his lips near her ear as he swayed her back and forth in his arms. He pressed his hands on her lower back, sending a warm sensation up her spine.

As they swayed and turned together, she caught sight of

Calen and Nina dancing together near the end of the row of seats where they were sitting earlier.

Emma couldn't tear her eyes away. Admittedly, a lot of years had passed since that high school dance, but this side of Calen she'd never seen before. The guy had moves and was kind of sexy. When did he learn to dance like that? And Nina had no problem keeping up.

She about gawked when Nina turned her back to Calen, lifted her arm, and put her hand behind his neck with her face tilted up just so. And then Calen ran his hand up her arm with his chin tucked in to look down at her with his other hand on her waist.

They looked like Baby and Johnny from Dirty Dancing. So cute…and so intimate…

"Hey, where'd you go?" Manny's voice snapped her back. He'd lifted his head and stared at her with that cute frown.

"Sorry." She shot a glance at Calen and Nina. "Just glad to see Calen and Nina hitting it off so well."

He followed her gaze. "Yeah, Nina's great. They seem to be a good fit."

"Yeah, they do."

He studied her face. "What's wrong?"

She blinked. "Nothing. Why do you ask?"

"Well, that cute smile of yours looks more like a frown right now, and you can't seem to stop watching them."

She snapped her attention back to him. "Sorry." She forced a short laugh. "I've never seen Calen dance like that. Kind of surprised me."

He frowned. "I thought you two went to a dance together way back when?"

"Yes, but Calen was so nervous he kept tripping on his own feet."

Manny chuckled. "Then I guess he's learned a few things since then."

"I guess so."

He pulled her close again. They continued to dance when the song changed to another angst-filled melody, swaying and turning. Emma laid her cheek against Manny's shoulder and tried to relax. But every time they made a full circle, she wound up searching for Calen and Nina.

At one point, her search located them farther back behind the seats where string lights from across the green sent enough of a glow to highlight their silhouettes.

They stood facing each other. Calen lowered his head to kiss Nina.

An ache bloomed in Emma's chest…

What would it feel like to be kissed by her best friend?

Chapter Eight

"For someone who says she's in love, you're acting more like Manny dumped you. Did something happen?"

Sheridan's statement snapped her attention to the present and out of her memory album from last night. For some reason, as many images of Calen and Nina dancing together—and kissing—filled this one compared to her and Manny. That should make her happy but for some reason it didn't.

Emma put her fork down. Even having brunch with her oldest and best friend didn't seem to lift this weird funk. "No, we're great. I think I'm just tired."

"Well, your classes did just finish." Sheridan poked around at her salad, probably searching for the rest of the bacon in her Cobb salad. She always started with the bacon.

The familiarity of being with Sheridan helped calm the small bubble of anxiety that she woke up with this morning. Had to be the stress of getting ready for this show. If she hadn't promised Calen she'd do it, she probably would be on the phone with the gallery owners to back out.

Noah walked out the front entrance of Madilyn's Grill & Wine Bar and headed toward their table on the patio. Their wedding was just a few weeks away and Emma still had to plan Sheridan's bachelorette party. She may have forgotten about that when she promised Calen she'd do the art show.

Her stress bubble expanded a bit.

Breathe, Emma. Calen's voice swooped into her thoughts yet again and overrode the threatening anxiety.

Emma wiped her mouth with her napkin and then pointed in the direction behind Sheridan. "Here comes your fiancé. Bet you love calling him that."

The sparkle in her friend's grin said it all. "Am I that obvious?"

Emma answered with a snort as Noah set a plate in the middle of the table.

"A little *amuse-bouche* from a certain kitchen elf." He stood back, looking rather pleased.

Emma gasped. "They're so cute!" The two ceramics spoons each held a mushroom cap filled with some kind of stuffing with a dollop of foam on top. "Did you make these?"

"No, Manny did. But I may have had a hand in some of the execution."

Sheridan grasped his forearm. "Well done, babe."

Noah leaned over to kiss her.

Emma giggled, happy for once not to be green with envy over Sheridan's happiness. She studied the plate, appreciating the presentation. "Yeah, nicely done, but what are they?"

"Baby portabellas filled with a crab, shrimp, and pancetta stuffing. And topped with a truffled cream foam."

Sheridan looked up at Noah. "Is this something new we're adding?"

Noah shrugged. "Maybe for special reservation groups, but I think this is more about Manny wanting to impress his girlfriend."

Girlfriend. Emma couldn't help but smile. No doubt the warmth in her cheeks signaled a serious blush. She loved the sound of it almost as much as she'd loved the sound of *fiancée*, but she'd rein in her bridal horses for now and live vicariously through Sheridan.

And Manny had somehow picked up on her love of mushrooms. She chose a spoon and brought it to her nose. Mushroom, garlic, and some kind of seasoning combination she couldn't identify brought a rush of saliva. She put the small bite-sized wonder into her mouth and chewed, releasing a myriad of flavors on her palate individually before combining into one glorious taste that left her wanting more.

She savored the bite a little longer before swallowing. "Wow, that's amazing."

Sheridan's eyes grew round as she chewed and swallowed. "I agree. Manny outdid himself."

With a backward glance, Noah picked up the plate. "You can tell the chef yourself, as he's heading this way."

Noah left the table and punched fists with Manny as they passed each other.

Once at their table, Manny leaned over and kissed Emma. "Hmmm, maybe a little too much salt."

Emma giggled and tugged on the front of his chef's jacket to bring him close again. "I think they're perfect."

He kissed her again, lingering this time before he pulled back. "I agree."

"All right, you two. People are trying to eat here." Humor filled Sheridan's scolding.

Manny grinned and gave her a quick bow of the head. "Duly noted, Madam Boss. I will return to my kitchen."

Sheridan rolled her eyes. "And don't let Chef Margot hear you call it your kitchen."

Emma grabbed his hand to give it a squeeze before he left, which he promptly lifted to his lips for a kiss. She didn't look away until he disappeared into the kitchen.

"You're a goner, aren't you?" Sheridan knew her better than anyone.

Except for Calen, of course.

"Yes, I think I am." Her smile made her cheeks hurt.

Sheridan studied her for a moment. "Okay, I have a confession to make."

Fork full and midway to her mouth, Emma paused, waiting for her to continue.

"I had a chat with Manny when you two first started dating."

"A chat?"

Sheridan hunched her shoulders toward her head. "More like a threat."

Emma put her fork down. "What did you do?"

"I told him if he broke your heart, I'd break him."

She didn't know whether to hug, laugh, or yell at her best friend. "Why?"

"Because he's a bit of a player, and I didn't want to see you get hurt. But I was wrong and I'm sorry. He's clearly nuts about you. I've never seen him this way before."

Emma buzzed from the tips of her toes all the way up to her neck. "Really?"

Sheridan did a quick nod. "Totally. Have you told him yet how you feel?"

She poked at her salad. "No, not like a blatant statement or anything like that. I don't want to scare him away."

"Maybe it's time to be honest and tell him how you feel."

Emma's stomach fluttered at the thought. "Maybe. I don't know."

She sat back in her seat and glanced toward Java Jerry's. Calen's familiar head stood out. He was actually sitting at one of his own tables, chatting with someone. She leaned forward, waiting for a glimpse of who sat across from him. Calen shifted, revealing Nina's familiar face, smiling...and flirting.

Her stomach did a lurch as she glanced away. Maybe the amuse-bouche hadn't agreed with her.

Sheridan twisted around in her seat. "Looks like love is definitely in the air."

"So it would seem." She put her fork down.

"And the funk is back." Sheridan sent a studious frown her way.

Emma wished Sheridan hadn't noticed. How could she explain what she didn't understand herself?

Sheridan crossed her arms as she sat back, looking more like Emma's interrogator instead of her best friend. "Care to enlighten me?"

Her friend's scrutiny made her want to squirm in her seat, but she resisted. "About what?"

"That reaction you just had to Calen and Nina being together."

"No reaction. I'm glad they're hitting it off."

"Is that what you call it? Because I would call it something else."

"Don't be silly. Calen's my best friend. I just don't want to see him get hurt."

Sheridan glanced their way again. "I've only met Nina a couple of times, but she seems great. If you thought she might hurt Calen, then why did you set them up?"

"Oh, I think she's great for him." She did her best to sound positive, but even she could hear the hesitancy in her voice.

Sheridan leaned her elbows on the table and tilted her head. "Your words say one thing, but that funk is telling me something else now."

"Sheri, stop looking for drama where there is none. I'm in love with Manny. And you're right. I should tell him." An idea popped into her head. "And I know exactly how I'm going to do it."

Here he sat with a beautiful woman, who even shared his love for Shakespeare, yet his brain seemed to want to jump ship and steal glimpses of Emma sitting across the street.

That ode to the fickleness of love beckoned his pen, but he refused. That would mean acknowledging he had a thing for Emma again and he refused to give it life.

Probably why he called Nina on a whim this morning and invited her to coffee. Seemed like the thing to do after their evening together in the park. And then their convo in the parking lot…he held no doubts regarding Nina's interest in him.

He just couldn't figure out what held him back from jumping fully in.

And everything was going great until he noticed Emma sitting with Sheridan. Anytime he caught a movement in his periphery vision, he had to look and see what she was doing. But then it got worse. Manny showed up and Emma lit up like a firecracker.

His stolen glance was so obvious that time that Nina even turned in her seat to check out what had grabbed his attention.

Busted.

Calen scrambled to think of something to say. "Guess we all like the same part of town."

That was all he could think of? How much lamer could he get?

Nina studied him a moment, then raised both brows to match her silent "oh." She put her hands flat on the table. "Now I get it."

Calen pretended to be distracted by the muffin they were sharing. "Get what? My love for banana nut muffins? There's one bite left. But hey, I know the owner and I'm pretty sure I could talk him into letting us have another one. On the house."

She reached out and clasped his hand. "Hey, it's okay. I get it. I've been in that place too."

"What place?"

Nina nodded her head in Emma's direction. "You've got a thing for her."

"No, I don't. And why does everyone keep saying that?"

She covered her mouth to hide her laugh. "Maybe because it's so obvious to everyone but you."

He couldn't move. Just stared at Nina while his brain scrambled for a reason why she might think he had a crush on his best friend. Because he'd used them all before, hadn't he? To protect Emma, to look out for Emma, to make sure Emma didn't fall too hard this time. He'd gotten really good at being Emma's protector. Of course, that would create a stronger bond, right?

But at that moment, Calen Cooper's heart turned traitor, and fessed up. All those feelings he thought he'd carefully locked away and assumed they'd fade away burst out of the vault and made a mess of his life.

He *did* have a thing for Emma. More than a thing if he allowed himself to acknowledge the tattered mess in his head. A month ago, he would have sworn up and down that he left that school boy crush behind in the halls of their high school, but had he really ever gotten over Emma? She'd never fallen this hard for anyone before, so how could he really be sure?

He leaned on the table and held his head in his hands. What did he do now? He lowered his arms and met Nina's eyes. Thankfully, he didn't see any judgment there. Just compassion.

"Wow, you've got it bad." She popped the last bite of muffin into her mouth. "Have you ever told her how you feel?"

He shook his head. "No reason to. I had a crush on her in high school, but she wasn't interested and so I settled into the friend zone."

"Settled *into* or settled *for*?"

"Is there a difference?"

"Yeah, a big one. *Into* means you've let go of the possibility of something more."

"I did!"

"No, you settled *for*. Trust me. Been there and burned the T-shirt."

He wanted to slam his fist down on the table, but that would do nothing but draw attention to his miserable self. And what about Nina? If he was going to be completely honest, he'd used her in an attempt to make those feelings go away.

"I'm sorry, Nina."

"For what?"

"For being an idiot who didn't realize the fickleness of his own heart. I'd totally understand if you left right now."

She glanced down at the empty plate. "Go get that muffin and let's talk about it."

"Seriously?"

"Totally. You need a friend right now and I fit the bill. See? That's settling into the friend zone." Her smile brought a smidge of relief to his anguish.

"Yeah, yeah. One muffin coming up." He pushed his chair back and stood.

He really could use a friend right now.

Chapter Nine

Talking things out with Nina had definitely helped. She had a way of bringing clarity to the situation. And broke things down in two directions. Either he did the "settle into" the friendship zone for real this time...

Or be honest with Emma and tell her how he felt. At least then, he'd get it out of his head—and his heart—and on the table. That way, if Emma decided she didn't return his feelings, which he was almost one hundred percent sure she didn't, he could move on.

But part of him still felt paralyzed to commit to a direction. Telling her that he might be in love with her while she was a smitten kitten might annihilate their friendship. He couldn't imagine his life without Emma, so he still had to weigh his options.

However, his longing for Emma seemed to be on an upward trajectory, but he landed on a temporary solution for the moment. And that was all about her art debut. He wanted that for her more than anything. Throwing his growing feelings into the mix right now might send her off the deep end, so he'd have to wait and risk her falling totally in love with Manny. And he with her.

At least he had a margin of relief in deciding. That alone made it easier for him to focus on the immediate tasks of getting ready for the show.

And today's task was to show Emma the T-shirts Kaleena had made for the Java Jerry's crew to promote the pre-show event he would launch on Facebook as soon as she knew about it. He'd carefully kept his plans a secret, and now he couldn't wait to see her reaction.

Emma would love it.

He'd texted her earlier and found out she had a new class starting tonight. His plan was to come near the end, help her clean up, and then share his surprise, starting with the T-shirt. Leaving the shop in the hands of his capable staff, he grabbed one of the shirts and walked over to Emma's studio.

Her voice carried out into the hallway. "Now that you've prepped your canvas, start imagining what you want to paint. You'll be surprised at how many ideas may come now that the white canvas can't intimidate you any longer. Let loose and have some fun."

Soft laughter followed her words as he stepped into the room. She had a full class this evening. Every easel had a student at work, filling the place with scratch-like sound as brushes moved across canvases.

Emma noticed his arrival and walked over. "Hey there. What brings you by?"

He did a casual shrug to keep the mystery going. "Oh, nothing really. Just thought I'd check out your new class; see if you needed any help."

She grinned. "How thoughtful. Thanks."

"And I might just have a little surprise for you."

Her brows lifted as her eyes lit up. "Oh? Do tell."

Calen unfurled the T-shirt, showing her the back. The design he'd created for the event came out better than he'd expected.

And judging by Emma's gasp, he'd succeeded. "Wow! Calen, I love it. Wait, this is the day before the actual show."

"Right. I talked to the gallery owners and proposed a pre-show event to help get the word out for opening night. They loved it. Java Jerry's will do the hosting, serving gourmet coffee drinks, fresh pastries and sweets from the bakery, and wine, which Noah and Sheridan contributed. My team and I will wear these from now on and at the event."

Tears puddled in the bottom of her eyes, reminding him of the ocean on a clear day. "I can't believe you did this. For me." She threw her arms around his neck and hugged him tighter than he could remember her ever doing.

"I told you I'd help in any way I can. Whatever you need, Emma." He drew back, but she didn't seem ready to let go, so he moved his arms around her again. The scent of her overwhelmed his senses. Her hair felt so soft against his cheek. If he didn't let go of her soon, he'd do something stupid.

"Am I interrupting something?" Manny's voice broke them apart.

Though his tone sounded humorous, Calen didn't miss the questioning look Manny sent his way.

Emma rushed over to show him the T-shirt. "Look at this. Calen planned this whole pre-show event for me. Isn't it amazing?" She glanced over her shoulder at Calen. "I still can't believe you did this."

Calen shrugged to downplay his immense pleasure at seeing Emma so happy with his surprise. That's what he'd wanted most, for her to be happy and excited about her debut. "Just doing my part."

Manny held out the bottom of the shirt and nodded his approval. "This is great. And it makes my surprise even better. When I worked in New York and LA, I got to know a few art critics who frequented the restaurants I worked in. I reached out and invited them to your show. Two of them are coming, just to see your work."

Emma squealed so loud she caught the attention of her students. She dropped the shirt as she jumped up and down before launching herself into Manny's arms.

Calen's joy took a nose dive along with the T-shirt. Right into the unknown abyss of Manny's shadow. He leaned over and grabbed the shirt before Emma's left shoe landed on it again and draped it over her desk chair.

Several of the students crowded around Emma to congratulate her as Manny brought up information about the critics on his phone.

Calen debated leaving but didn't want to just disappear like that. Emma might think he was upset or something, which he kind of was. Well, maybe a lot. Staying took every bit of his willpower, actually. But he kept telling himself what mattered most was Emma's happiness. He could ride out this scenario.

Maybe…

An older gentleman walked over and stood by him. "This is a huge opportunity for Emma."

"Yeah, it is." He tucked his fingers into the top of his jean pockets.

"I could tell your surprise meant a lot to her, too."

Calen studied the man. He seemed familiar.

He held his hand out. "Norman Kent. Noah's dad."

Calen reciprocated the shake. "We met at the engagement party, right?"

Norman quirked a smile and raised his brows at Calen. "It was a big hit."

Calen chuckled, appreciating Norman's double entendre. "Saw that, did you?"

"Everyone did, but I'm guessing things worked out."

He swung his attention back to Emma and Manny and deflated his lungs. "That's one way of looking at it."

―――――――――

The best day ever. That's how Emma would label her memory file of today. First Calen with his surprise—she didn't get to thank him again because he left in all the commotion, leaving a message with Norman that he had to get back to his shop. She made a mental note to call him on her way home.

And then Manny's big surprise. That he would do something like that to help her left her breathless in a whole new way. She couldn't wait to see him again after his shift at the restaurant.

Tonight would be the night. The night she would tell him she was in love with him. After what he did for her—to actually seek out art critics to attend the show for her benefit —that had to mean he loved her too.

Why else would he do such a generous thing like that?

She dropped into her seat at her desk and stared at the circle of easels. Even her students had celebrated with her. At this rate, her memory banks would burst with an overflow of gratitude. Her dreams were finally coming true.

A great guy in her life, who seemed to return her affection in equal amount.

Her career was about to launch to a whole new level.

Even her creativity and productivity had increased substantially. Most likely because of Manny. He'd become her muse.

Something poked her back. She turned around and tugged the T-shirt into her lap and then spread it out on her desk.

Calen…he was her rock. He'd believed in her before anybody else. She really needed to talk to him and make sure he knew that.

"You've had quite a night."

She spun around.

Norman stood in the doorway. "Sorry to disturb you, but I got to my car and realized I forgot my bag."

Emma grabbed the sack she'd found earlier from under her desk. "I thought this might be yours."

He walked over and took it from her. "Thanks."

"Are you enjoying the class? Not too basic for you, I hope. Sheridan said you're an amazing painter."

Norman gave her a shy smile. "She's very generous with her praise. I'm self-taught, so I'm looking forward to learning the proper way to prep a canvas and other things I'm sure I need to know."

Emma rose from her seat. "Well, I'm happy to help you any way I can."

He hesitated for a moment. "He really cares about you, doesn't he?"

A surge of pleasure rushed through her body. "Yeah, he does. Manny's amazing. I never expected that he'd do something like that."

Norman pointed to the T-shirt on her desk. "I meant Calen. He's really fond of you."

She picked up the shirt and held it against her

abdomen. "He and Sheridan are my best friends. I can't imagine my life without them."

"Really? He's just a friend? Sure seemed like more than that to me. But what do I know? I'm an old man." He chuckled at himself, then held up the bag. "See you next week."

Something seemed afoot. "Norman?"

He stopped at the doorway and turned around. "Yeah?"

"Did you really forget your bag?"

"Perhaps." He grinned, then continued on his way.

She didn't move. Just stood there, staring at the empty doorway as she let Norman's words settle in. Sheridan had mentioned her future father-in-law had a 'wise way' about him. Her words. Emma didn't get it then, but she did now.

She replayed the evening's events in her head. How excited Calen was to tell her about his surprise—she held up the T-shirt—something he'd clearly worked on for weeks.

And then Manny showed up, and well, interrupted Calen, come to think of it. She was so swept away by Manny's surprise that she didn't get back to Calen's.

Now she felt like an ungrateful friend. She picked up her phone and tapped his face on her favorites list, but the call went right to his message after one ring.

Maybe he was on the phone with Nina. She checked the time. He was probably getting ready to close the coffee shop. She could go over and thank him properly.

After grabbing her bag—and the T-shirt—she locked her studio and drove over to the shop so she'd have her car nearby. Most of the retail shops had closed already, having adopted summer hours now that tourist season had dwindled. Only the restaurants and Java Jerry's stayed open past six or seven for the evening dinner crowds. She parked and grabbed the T-shirt, slipping it over her tank top to surprise Calen.

The open sign was off and only a few lights lit the interior of the shop. Calen sat on the couch near the front.

She lifted her hand to knock on the glass but stopped when Nina approached and sat down next to him. Nina cupped his face and leaned in to kiss him, which Calen seemed a willing participant.

Something hitched in Emma's chest. Whatever Norman saw, she couldn't imagine it being more than friendship. How could it be if Calen was involved with Nina like that?

But for a moment, her heart had pondered the idea of Calen having more than 'friendly' feelings for her, and... she'd liked it. More than she should. After all, didn't she love Manny?

Not wanting to disrupt Calen's date, she turned away to head back to her car.

The sound of the door opening stopped her.

She turned around as Calen stopped on the sidewalk. "Hey, I didn't know you were coming by. Did we have something planned?"

"No, I just wanted to come by and thank you again." She held out the bottom of the shirt. "I really love that you did this for me. It's wonderful."

He tucked his hands into his jean pockets and shrugged. "I know it's not as big a deal as having known art critics come to your show, but—"

"It's a big deal, Calen." She closed the distance between them. "Especially to me. I couldn't do any of this without you."

He smiled before glancing over his shoulder to where Nina stood inside.

"Sorry, I didn't mean to interrupt your date."

"That's okay. We're just hanging out. You can join us if you'd like."

Emma glanced at Nina, who continued to watch them. "No, I think you two should enjoy your time without a third wheel. I'm meeting Manny after he's done working anyway."

"Right. Great. You two have fun." His smile flattened before he started to turn around.

"Calen?"

He spun back around. "Yeah?"

She didn't plan to do it—her body seemed to take on a mind of its own. That's the only way she could describe what she did next. She strode to where he stood and hugged him—the big hug kind that left no space between them.

Calen hesitated at first but then wrapped his arms around her. Nina would probably cross-examine her about it later, but she'd reassure that it was nothing more than friendship.

But not like this, said a tiny voice inside of her. And that part of her noticed how his hands pressed her against him and how his face lowered enough that she could hear his breath against her ear.

She'd only ever kissed Calen once, and that was on the cheek at that horrible high school dance where her date had dumped her. And that was to thank him for being there for her. For being her best friend.

She didn't know what possessed her to do it again now, but she did. Emma held his arms as she kissed his cheek. The smell of roasted coffee beans filled her nose, along with the underlying scent of sandalwood. She'd have to explain that to Nina too, but she needed Calen to know how much she appreciated and cared for him.

"Thanks again." She mumbled the words as she made a

dash for her car to drive away, not letting herself even look at him.

Because something felt different that time, felt like more than just a thank you. She didn't know what exactly, only that the feel of his cheek against hers and the scent of him lingered as she drove away.

Chapter Ten

Calen stood on the sidewalk, waiting for Emma's brake lights to go off as she turned down the street. The feel of her lingered in his mind and on his body. Something had definitely changed between them, but was that just him, or did she sense his feelings for her?

He went back inside the coffee shop and locked the door. Nina sat in the corner of the couch with her legs tucked up next to her, sipping from the cup of tea he'd made her.

He ran a hand through his hair, unsure of how to approach what happened between him and Nina before Emma showed up. He thought they'd clarified their relationship moving forward would be a friendship. Had Nina changed her mind?

"What was that about?"

Nina put her cup down. "You mean the kiss, I presume."

"Yes, unless you want to talk about something else, but in my mind, the kiss would be the higher priority."

"And which kiss are you referring to? Mine or Emma's?" She quirked her brows up just so to match her wry grin.

"Yours, of course." No way would he discuss what had just happened between him and Emma. Not until he processed it himself.

She covered her mouth as she giggled. "I just wanted to help things along."

He tilted his head in thought. "Things between us?"

"No, between you and Emma, you dork. I saw her walking up and made the most of it."

"There is no *thing* between Emma and me." Maybe if he kept saying that, it would go away. Worked back in high school, hadn't it?

"Not yet. Thus why I'm trying to help it along." Her voice lilted with sarcastic emphasis.

"How? By trying to make her jealous or something?"

"No, but that could help." She unfolded her legs and sat forward. "Look, you and Emma have been best friends for years, and based on what you've shared with me, she'd never seen you in a serious relationship."

He pulled his head back. "I date."

She rolled her eyes. "I'm not talking about a date here and there. There's a difference between her knowing you date and actually seeing you in a romantic relationship, like having a girlfriend."

"Okay, I get that. But you and I aren't dating. I thought we clarified that."

"Right, but Emma doesn't know that."

"Yeah, so?"

"So what's the harm in letting her think that and see what happens?"

"You mean like a fake relationship?" Why did his voice

go up an octave? And he had no desire to lie to Emma. "I can't lie to her."

"Start tracking with me here, Cooper. We're not. We're just two friends who hang out and might be more in her eyes."

"In her eyes? And what about yours, Nina?" No point in leading her on. He'd seen the heartache Emma had endured. He couldn't do that to someone else.

She held her hand up. "Hey, I'm just a friend helping another friend in this scenario. I'm good."

He dropped onto the couch and held his head. Was he actually considering this? "This is nuts. And it'll never work. She's totally in love with Manny."

"Right, I get that, but you might be surprised how seeing you involved in a romantic light might give her pause for thought."

He lifted his head. "Pause for thought? I'm not sure I want to be anyone's *pause*."

Nina laughed. "You're funny."

"Another stellar compliment to my ego." His voice turned deadpan.

She slid over and put her hand on his knee. "If you're not comfortable with the idea, I get it. But I'm putting it out there. I don't mind being your fake love interest if it helps."

Hearing her name it made him want to shudder. Like watching some of those romcoms Emma loved. "I'll think about it."

"Okay." She picked up her tea and took a sip. "I can be pretty convincing, by the way."

"I said, I'll consider it."

"Good." She held her cup out to him. "And you can thank me with more tea."

In the short time she had left before Manny's expected arrival, Emma took down the easels and arranged the lounger near the window in her studio so they could look at the moon. She didn't have much time, so she drove down the street to the closest drugstore and grabbed some candles, a bottle of sparkling cider, some plastic champagne glasses, and a couple types of chocolate truffles that she knew Manny liked.

Back at her studio, she dragged a small table to sit by the lounger and draped it with a scarf she found stuffed in the box of items she used for her drawing classes. Then she arranged the plastic flutes, the bottle of cider, and the chocolates in front of the lit candles.

Hands on her hips, she stepped back to assess her work. Not exactly a fancy restaurant, but she couldn't think of a better place to tell Manny she loved him than where their relationship began.

She checked the time. Manny would be any minute, which left her enough time to duck into the bathroom and change. She'd brought the cute sundress that Manny seemed to like a lot and a pair of her wedges. With a refresh of her makeup, she swept her hair up into a twist, leaving soft tendrils to flutter down around her face.

As she walked back into her studio, she smelled roses. A huge red bouquet—at least two dozen, maybe three—stood in a glass vase on her desk.

She gasped and dipped her nose in to inhale their sweet scent. "They're beautiful. And so many!"

Manny gestured to the table and candles. "Great minds think alike."

"Oh?" She stepped into the circle of his arms and met his lips. Light at first, but then more passionate. As if he needed her to know something.

Her memory album of past breakups fluttered open and reminded her of the one who brought her red roses to say he loved her but not in that way. Then kissed her goodbye. He thought the roses would soften the blow. She'd tossed them in the dumpster.

Was Manny about to break up with her? Her chest tightened as she pulled away and her heartbeat shifted into overdrive. She closed her eyes and focused on her breathing.

"Emma, what's wrong?" He sat down on the lounger and tugged her down with him.

She put her hand on his chest to stop him when he tried to pull her close again.

"I, uh, I just need a moment." Maybe she'd misread him…and blown the entire evening. Why did her body have to do this to her now? She pictured the bird feeder hanger Calen had made for her and inhaled deeply, then exhaled.

"Did I do something wrong?" His hurt tone snapped her eyes open. He searched her face, while his own conveyed his deep concern.

She forced a smile and squeezed his hand. If she wanted a genuine relationship with him, she needed to know she could be real about her anxiety issue. Maybe Manny would be the one who didn't run away.

"No, the roses are beautiful." She cupped his face. "Sometimes I have these attacks. Panic attacks."

He nodded. "I understand. My sister dealt with those as a child."

A small sense of relief flooded through her. Understanding was most of the battle. "I did too. They happen less now that I'm an adult. Just when I feel overwhelmed."

He held her hands as he shifted to face her. "The roses, were they too much? I wanted to show you in a big way how much I care about you, Emma."

The tightness in her chest relaxed. So far so good. Why stop being honest now? She ran one hand down his arm as tears burned her eyes. "I thought you were breaking up with me."

He chuckled with his smile and tucked a tendril of hair behind her ear. "No, not at all." His expression turned nervous. "Quite the opposite." He cleared his throat as he dropped his gaze to their still clasped hands before returning to search her face. "I've never felt about anyone like I feel about you, Emma. I'm falling for you."

Her sudden intake of breath preceded her full-on launch into his arms that sent them both back onto the lounger in a passionate kiss.

She pushed away and stared at him. Had he really said it first? That he loved her? Here she'd planned and agonized over telling him how she felt and he beat her to the confession.

More tears blurred her vision. She blinked until she could see him clearly again. "I love you too."

Acutely aware that she was lying almost on top of him, she lowered her head, intending to kiss him in a way that conveyed everything in her heart. Tender, slow, caring… loving and intimate.

Manny slid his arms around her back and shifted them both so they were side-by-side on the lounger. He brushed the curve of her chin with his lips and nuzzled into her neck. "I love the smell of you."

His lips trailed a path back to her mouth, and the kiss turned more demanding and urgent. At one point, Emma had to pull away to catch her breath.

All of this was happening so fast.

But wasn't this what she always wanted? Longed for?

He hovered over her, devouring her with his dark eyes. "Tell me what you want."

She started to speak, then stopped. What was he really asking her? About *this* moment and what happened next? Or every moment after this one? He'd been honest and expressed his feelings for her. How could she do less if she wanted a future with this man?

And so far, he'd given her every indication he was serious. First, by wanting to be exclusive and now confessing his love even before she did.

"I'm not interested in a short romance, Manny. I want something serious that's leading to a possible future. Are you okay with that?"

He touched the tip of her nose with his. "More than okay."

She cupped his face and kissed him. "Just one more thing."

He leaned back some to study her face. "Yes?"

"Will you be my plus one at Sheridan's wedding?"

A soft chuckle accompanied his smile. "I'm already going."

"Yes, but if you're my plus one, you'll sit with me at the wedding party table." She didn't want to say it, but really and truly, this was about making it clear to the rest of the world that Manny Silva was involved in a serious relationship.

In other words, TAKEN.

She didn't miss the way women looked at him and the flirtatious way he reacted sometimes. Sheridan had told her he was a bit of a player, and though Emma wasn't convinced that was completely true, she wanted just a little reassurance, some protection for her battle-weary heart.

His smile faltered for a moment, but then spread wide, bringing a twinkle to his eyes. "Then I officially accept your invitation, Emma Price."

Chapter Eleven

Emma stared at Sheridan's wedding dress as she stood on the platform in the bridal shop fitting room. With her wedding just under a month away, today was all about final tweaks and alterations. They had a full day of wedding stuff planned that Emma barely fit into her schedule along with maintaining her private art classes—her main income over the summer—and working on her pieces for the art show that landed a couple of weeks after Sheridan's big day.

Sheridan had shown her the tux they'd chosen for Noah. And, of course, Emma's imagination ran wild, picturing Manny in a tux. She blushed as she remembered their evening together—sharing their dreams and aspirations for the future and several passionate kisses. They'd talked well past midnight, and she—being more tired than she realized—fell asleep with her head on his chest on the lounger.

She felt so safe with him. So loved and protected. When she woke up in the morning, Manny was already gone. But he'd left a single rose by her with a note that said, "I'll be thinking about us all day."

"Emma!"

She met Sheridan's stern expression in the floor-to-ceiling mirror. "Yeah?"

"I called your name four times. Are you okay?"

"Yeah, totally."

Sheridan's face softened as she tilted her head in concern. "You look exhausted. What happened last night?"

She didn't stop the smile that spread so wide her cheeks hurt. "Manny told me he loved me last night."

Her friend gasped and leaned over to hug her, which forced the seamstress pinning her dress to stop and lean back so as not to get stuck. "Oh, sorry!" She positioned herself back on the platform, facing Emma's reflection. "I'm so glad you finally told him how you feel."

She felt like a balloon filled with paint, about to burst in glorious color onto a canvas—one of her experimental phases. "He said it first."

Sheridan's expression reminded her of the figure in Edvard Munch's *The Scream*. "Seriously?!"

Emma bobbed her head. "I know, right? What's crazy is at first I totally thought he was about to break up with me, but he was just nervous about telling me how he felt."

"Just like you were about telling him."

"Exactly. It was…amazing. We kissed and talked until like three this morning and fell asleep on the lounger in my studio."

"Just kissed and talked?" Sheridan sounded skeptical.

"Manny doesn't want to rush me." She lowered her voice. "When I thought he was breaking up with me, I started to have a panic attack, so I had to tell him why. That they hit me when I feel overwhelmed or upset."

"How did he handle it?"

"He said his sister dealt with them as a child, so he understood. Then he was concerned that he'd overwhelmed me." She giggled. "He was so cute."

"Wow. Way to go Manny. I'm impressed."

"Me too." She moved closer to where Sheridan stood. "I told him I want a future with him and he said he felt the same way."

Sheridan blinked and raised her brows. "Wow. If I wasn't stuck on this platform, I'd be hugging you again."

Emma wrapped her arms around herself and sighed. "Can you mark him as my plus one so he can sit at the wedding party table?"

"I thought you were planning to ask Calen?"

She fiddled with the satin strap on her dress. Sheridan had picked a luscious shade of dark olive green for the maid of honor gown, knowing how much Emma loved greens. "That was before I was seeing anyone. He'll understand."

"Why don't you tell Calen to still come and bring Nina? I'll add her to the list. That way, you don't run the risk of him feeling hurt."

"Okay, I guess that would work."

"You guess? Unpack that one for me."

"I don't even know if Nina and Calen are a thing."

"Are you kidding? Did you not see them dancing together the other night? I'm pretty sure they're an item, Emma."

And she'd seen them kissing last night when she went looking for Calen at his shop. "You're probably right."

As the seamstress finished, Sheridan stepped down from the platform and rested her hands on Emma's forearms. "It's a perfect solution. You'll have your boyfriend and your best friend to keep you company while I'm totally distracted by my new husband."

She laughed as Sheridan ducked into one of the dressing rooms to change back into her clothes while Emma took her turn on the platform. The seamstress worked at the back of her gown to raise the length just above the heels she'd purchased for the event. The front of the dress swept up to a point mid-thigh on the right side. She would ask Manny to make sure his tux complemented her dress so they'd look amazing together, dancing at the reception.

Noah and Manny seemed like good friends. How cool would it be if she married her best friend's husband's best friend? They could hang out at each other's places having dinner and playing games. She and Sheridan could plan to get pregnant at the same time so their kids could grow up together. They could even take family vacations together.

Maybe she'd be the one to catch the bouquet. She could picture that, too. And Manny's kiss as he hinted at making her his bride.

Yes, it would all be so perfect.

And if things worked out between Nina and Calen, he would have his own happy ending, too.

Calen stared at the text from Emma again, then leaned back against the counter near the espresso machine. Part of him understood. She and Manny were an item now, and it made sense that she'd want him to be her date at Sheridan's wedding.

And he could see Sheridan adding Nina as his plus one as being thoughtful and giving him a chance to have a good time at the wedding with his new "love" interest.

Emma's words…

He read the last line of her text again.

This is what you want, right?

What he wanted at that exact moment was to throw his phone at the back wall of the shop. The brick facade would do a marvelous job pulverizing it and Emma's message. If only he could do that with these feelings about Emma. He should be thrilled for his best friend. Why did this old junk from the past have to rear its ancient historical head now?

So far, Nina's plan—more of an idea—to make Emma think they were an item was succeeding, but that put him in a terrible place of having to keep up the lie until after Sheridan's wedding, or just telling Emma that it didn't work out. Which really wouldn't be a lie.

Instead of replying, he groaned his frustration, turned his phone off, and left it on the counter. If a hot coffee pot got placed on it or the espresso machine happened to overflow and leave it in a puddle, he could live with that.

Kaleena walked in for her usual afternoon coffee boost. "Hey there, my friend. How's your day going?"

Calen grabbed a cup to start her order and deadpanned his reply. "Fine and dandy."

She puckered her lips in a frown. "Ew, not like 'cotton candy' I'd say."

He snickered. "You got that right."

Kaleena glanced from side to side before leaning toward him over the counter. "Is this an Emma thing again?"

"You could say that." He started frothing the milk for her drink. The noise gave him a reprieve to gather his thoughts. He took Kaleena's drink over to the counter and rang up her order.

"Shop's kind of slow today. Come over for a chat if you want to later." Concern covered her face like a tragic theater mask. He didn't know all the details, but he knew Kaleena well enough to know she had firsthand experience with heartbreak.

"I'm okay, but thanks for the offer. I'll take a rain check though."

She smiled as she gave him money for her order, then picked up her cup. "Anytime. My door is always open for you, Calen."

Steph walked behind the counter and tossed the rag she'd been using to wipe down the tables into the disinfectant bucket. "You okay?"

He needed to do a better job of keeping his personal life out of the shop. Not good for business. "Yep, I'm good."

"Liar." She headed to the kitchen area with the tray of dirty mugs and plates she'd collected from the breakfast crowd.

The front door bells jingled and in walked Nina. She didn't say a word, just held her phone up. "Please tell me you got a text from Emma."

He swiped his phone from the counter. "Yep, sure did."

Nina rushed to the counter to whisper like a conspirator. "Our plan is working."

He grabbed Nina's hand and led her to his office so they could speak behind closed doors. "This isn't working at all. She thinks we're an item."

Nina blurted a frustrated snicker. "Well, duh, wasn't that our plan?"

"Your idea, and no, not like this. She's happy about it." He powered his phone back up and showed her the texts.

Nina scanned Emma's messages, which just made him feel slimy. She handed his phone back. "I'm not convinced she's happy about it."

"She even says, 'This is what you want, right?'"

"Exactly my point."

He did a double take. "Are we reading the same text?"

"What she's really asking is if you're sure I'm the one you want to be with."

Weren't they talking about the same thing? "Isn't that what I'm saying?"

"No, it's not about me. It's about you." Nina plopped down in his desk chair, looking rather pleased with herself. "She's trying to figure out if you're no longer an option."

"An option? What does that even mean?"

"It means our plan worked. Emma is starting to see you in a different light, and let me tell you from experience, when a best friend starts to see you that way, it's hard to resist."

Chapter Twelve

The back counter in her studio served as a great place to stage the paintings she'd done so far for the gallery showing. She'd created a theme to her paintings to show continuity, but each painting represented a captured moment. So far, her favorite was the one with Manny.

Emma had sketched him that day when he first sought her out, but the painting had captured his essence more than his form. Detailed areas captured his eyes and his smile, but only hints of detail composed the rest of his form. She'd brought in abstract elements to create what she hoped would convey a sense of chaos coming into order.

Which is what her life felt like these days. Mostly. Like everything she'd longed for was shifting into place. Finally. Even the gallery showing didn't scare her as much anymore. That, in and of itself, was a tremendous accomplishment in her mind.

She should share that with Calen. Without his nudge, aka pushiness, she never would have done it. And she'd gained so much more than a few new pieces of work for an art show.

Though not finished, she put the last two canvases next to the others to get a feel for the flow of her work so far. A surge of excitement and satisfaction zipped through her. She was going to pull this off after all.

"Knock, knock." Nina stood in the doorway, dressed in a beach cover-up that revealed the bright pink strings of her bathing suit tied around her neck. "I'm heading to the beach and thought I'd drop by. How's it going?" She pointed toward the paintings as she walked into the studio.

Hands on her hips, Emma stepped back and assessed her work so far. "Really good, actually."

Nina took a position next to her and studied the display. "Wow, Emma. This is some of your best work." She pointed to the one of Manny. "I love that one. You really captured his presence."

Emma beamed at her. "I love that one too." She studied the painting again. "He made it easy."

"He seems like a really great guy."

"He is. He's amazing. I love his passion for life." She dropped her arms and turned to Nina. "How are you and Calen doing?"

She tilted her head from side to side. "We're, uh, good. Having a good time, you know?"

"You two are so cute together."

Nina played with the tassels on the bottom of her beach cover-up. "Yeah, Calen's a really great guy. I like him."

"Do you just like him or do you *really* like him?" She liked Nina. Even considered her a good friend, but she didn't want Calen to get hurt.

Nina paused, studying her for a moment. "Why are you asking?"

Emma shrugged. "He's my best friend. I just want to make sure he doesn't get his heart ripped out."

Nina tucked her chin in and raised her brows. "Do you think I'm capable of doing that to him?"

"No, silly. Not on purpose. It's just, Calen can be really sensitive. He's a deep guy. It's the poet in him. He doesn't hold back when it comes to the people he cares about, and he doesn't take relationships lightly. I just wanted to be sure you two are on the same page."

"You sure that's all this is?" Nina crossed her arms.

"Yes, of course. Calen's always been there for me. I want to do the same for him."

Nina lowered her arms to her sides. "Okay, well, then yeah, I really like him. And I promise to be gentle with your best friend's heart. Does that make you feel better?"

"Sure." She smiled. That's what she wanted to hear, right? That Nina was as into Calen as he was into her. And he seemed to really like Nina. "I'm so excited that you'll be with Calen at Sheridan's wedding. Have you found a dress yet?"

"No, haven't even shopped yet."

"I can help you find a dress if you'd like."

"Sure, that would be great. Just not today." She patted her beach bag. "The beach and I already have a date."

A thought popped into Emma's mind. "Are you free tonight?"

"After a day in the sun, shopping is the last thing I want to do."

"No, I was going to invite you to movie night tonight. It's this thing Calen and I do once a week, although we haven't really had time lately. If you want to come, I can invite Manny, and we can all hang out." She wanted Manny and Calen to get to know each other better and now that

Calen and Nina were dating, he wouldn't feel like a third wheel or something.

Nina lowered her eyelids. "You don't think Calen will mind?"

"No, why would he mind? Do you think it's a bad idea?"

With a quick shake of her head, Nina lifted her hands. "No, not at all. I think it's a great idea."

―――――

"This is a really bad idea." Calen parked the car outside of Emma's apartment building but didn't get out. Not yet. He had to get his head in this weird game he and Nina had concocted. Well, mostly Nina.

"Are you kidding? This is going to be great. A more relaxed setting. Emma will see what romantic Calen is like on her home ground."

"Romantic Calen? Seriously? My strengths are sarcasm and vicious rhetoric, as the infamous Topher Grace said."

"Who?"

"It's from one of Emma's favorite romcoms. Never mind." He shook his head. "This is crazy, you know? I mean borderline ridiculous."

"No, I think it's sweet that you remember something from one of her favorite movies."

"No, not that. This." He wagged his hand between them. "It's a recipe for disaster."

Nina leaned her head back against the headrest. "Calen, will you just relax?" She twisted in her seat to face him. "How about this? Forget about trying to be romantic and leave that part up to me."

"What do you mean?"

"Just follow my lead. Okay?" She jumped out of the car before he could argue further.

Calen pushed out of the car and caught up with Nina on the sidewalk. "We need a signal."

She laughed. "For what? Why?"

"To let you know when I've had enough."

She grabbed his arm and brought him to a stop. "Okay, how about something cute between us so it won't look suspicious."

"Cute? Not sure I can do cute."

"Sexy then?"

"Noooooo."

She was having way too much fun with this.

"I know, I'll yawn." He raised his brows in anticipation of her answer.

"Lame and cliché." She paused in thought. "How about this?" She wrapped her arms around his waist and laid her head against his chest, just below his chin. "Now kiss my head."

"What?"

"Kiss my head. Just a quick one."

"Okay." He did as she commanded, because that's really what it was as far as he was concerned, and he blindly obeyed. "How's that?"

She pulled back and looked up at him. "Perfect, because Emma was watching us the whole time."

Instinct made him want to pull back, but Nina anticipated his move and held him in place. "I saw her watching for us in the window as we got out of the car. So keep your game face on because here she comes."

Emma stopped a few feet in front of them. She wore that cute, bright green jumper she liked to lounge around in and had her hair pulled up loosely on top of her head. "Hi, guys! Manny's making us gourmet popcorn for the movie. You two can snuggle up on the couch while we get the rest of our snacks ready."

She waved them to follow her as she spun around and hurried back into the apartment. Or was that a skip? Did Emma just skip up the step?

"This won't work."

"Why not?"

"She skipped."

"Yeah, so?"

"Emma told me once that she gave up skipping when her father left."

"Oh, that's...that's kind of sad."

"Yeah." He didn't move. Just stared at the step, remembering the little bounce she did up onto the step. She looked so...free.

Nina hooked her arm into his. "It'll be okay, Calen. I've got your back. And just squeeze my hand."

"Why?" He dropped his gaze to look at her.

"As the signal. Squeeze my hand if you need to bail."

Chapter Thirteen

Calen didn't miss the way Nina sat against him on the couch and tugged his arm over her shoulders. Nor the way she kept doing this cute snuggle-wiggle thing and would smile at him whenever he looked at her.

Definitely an Oscar-worthy performance for her.

Death for him if his insides continued to tie in knots.

Emma blew in from her kitchenette again, carrying another large bowl of popcorn and two cans of soda. She set them on the coffee table in front of them. "Oh shoot, I forgot the Sno-Caps."

Nina leaned forward and dug into her bag. "I brought peanut M&Ms."

"With popcorn?"

Emma said it at the same time he did, which made them both laugh and eased the tightness in his jaw. Maybe he could get through this evening after all. Nothing had really changed between him and Emma. They were and always would be best friends. He'd keep his head in the friend zone and avoid watching Manny and Emma together; like they were now. Working together in the kitchen to make food, entertaining guests—almost like playing house.

He clenched his jaw again.

After greeting Calen and Nina, Manny sat down on the other end of the couch in the corner, arm out for Emma to take her place next to him. Almost as if they'd done this many a time. Which they most likely had.

Calen did the math in his head. Emma hadn't dated anyone longer than a month or so. Not seriously. She and Charles had lasted a month if he counted the last week the creep ghosted her. This was why Calen wanted to punch out the coward but hit Manny by mistake.

Emma picked up the remote and turned on the TV.

Nina leaned forward, lifted their bowl of popcorn, and plopped it into his lap. Good thing it was a lightweight plastic bowl. "What movie are we watching?"

"The Chef." She beamed at Manny. "I figured that would be a great way to break Manny into our movie night routine."

Calen resisted rolling his eyes. Of course, Emma would pick a movie like that because of Manny.

"Awww, how sweet." Nina smiled up at him, but the mirth in her eyes spoke another reaction. She was actually enjoying his discomfort.

Manny leaned forward and smiled at Nina. "And next time, Nina can pick the movie."

Emma hit the button, and the movie started. She snuggled into Manny's side with her head and hand on his chest.

Calen hunkered down a smidge so that Nina's head rested closer to his and would block his periphery view of Emma and Manny.

About twenty minutes into the movie, a buzzer went off.

Manny shot off the couch while Emma paused the movie. "Are they ready, babe?"

Babe? She had a nickname for him now?

Emma's oven door creaked along with Manny's reply. "Yes, they're perfect."

More sounds of a tray sliding out of the oven and a plate clanking on the counter filtered into the living room. Then Manny, grinning ear to ear at his creation, walked in and then set the platter on the coffee table. Small pastry squares with something white and brown in the middle filled the plate. Sprigs of herbs dotted the tops.

"A trial run on a recipe I'm perfecting."

Nina leaned over and inhaled. "What is it?"

"Puff pastry with fig and goat cheese. And a little rosemary to finish it off." He popped one in his mouth and did a quick groan. "Better than I expected."

Emma nibbled on a corner, nodding her agreement, but Calen knew she hated goat cheese. Said it tasted furry to her.

Nina took a bite of hers and moaned. "That's amazing!"

"Right?" Manny beamed at her with a full set of pearly whites.

Calen shoved one in his mouth and had to admit, the man knew his appetizers. "Is this for Madilyn's?"

"No, for the art show preview you have planned."

"But I already have the appetizers planned out. We made a special order from the bakery to do some special petit fours and macaroons."

"The appetizers I have planned are savory and will level things up." Manny traced Emma's face with his finger and then kissed her. "Anything to help Emma's show be a success."

Emma crumpled her napkin, but Calen didn't miss that she didn't finish her piece.

"Manny's savories and your sweets, Calen, will be a perfect balance. Don't you think?" Emma's eyes pleaded with him to agree.

"Yeah, of course. That's a great idea."

Emma smiled at him. That smile she always gave him after he helped her with a panic attack. That smile that told him he'd said or done just the right thing when she needed it. *That* smile that said she loved him like a best friend and nothing more.

She lifted the remote and started the movie again.

Calen shoved a handful of popcorn in his mouth so he would have something to chomp down on other than his teeth.

Emma tried not to look. Seriously tried not to sneak glances at Nina and Calen.

Leaning forward to grab something from the coffee table helped mask her true intentions, even though it meant she had to eat another one of Manny's furry goat cheese concoctions. She'd become a master of camouflage in using her napkin to not only wipe her mouth but spit out her bites.

She almost breathed a sigh loud enough to hear when he brought out his second creation—a mushroom and aged Swiss arrangement that included some kind of toast crisp and smoked paprika. Which he attributed to Noah, who loved the stuff.

That one was right up her alley, and she probably ate most of them, using the movement to study Calen and

Nina's relationship. She'd made a pig of herself and her stomach roiled its agreement.

Why did she care so much about the dynamics of Calen's relationship with Nina, anyway? She'd told herself it was just to make sure Calen didn't get hurt, but now she had to wonder if it might be more. Was there something she sensed on a subconscious level that set off alarm bells? Or did she have a problem sharing her best friend? Which was ridiculous. She wanted Calen to be as happy as she was.

And she was happy.

She should focus on the movie, especially since she picked it for Manny's sake. Based on what he'd shared about the beginnings of his chef's career, John Favreau's character seemed like a winner. Manny sure seemed to enjoy it. He'd vocalized his agreements and criticisms at several of the cooking scenes.

Albeit his running commentary made hearing part of the dialogue difficult, which no doubt drove Calen batty. That she could tell without even looking at him. He loved to study the words used in dialogue for their unspoken meaning. Sometimes she loved their discussions about the movies more than the movies themselves.

She didn't realize the movie had ended until Manny nudged her with his elbow. "Emma? Where did you go?"

Emma put her hand on Manny's knee. "Sorry, just lost in thought for a moment."

He laughed and redirected his attention to Nina and Calen. "I think she left us to go into her little painter world."

Her little painter world...Manny had labeled her tendency to drift off thinking of techniques or ideas for the art show as her little painter world. She'd thought it was cute at first, but then sensed an underlying irritation that she wasn't focusing on him.

She turned away from Manny and caught Calen's frown. "Sorry about that. I'm here now." She forced a grin as she stacked the empty plates into the popcorn bowls along with the empty candy boxes.

Nina carried one into the kitchen. "I do it all the time. It's the fate of an artist." She added a flair of drama to her last statement.

Calen took the other bowl from Emma. "All artists do it. It's just part of who we are."

His hazel eyes relayed the message that he understood and didn't mind. He never did, because he did it too. They both did. Even together. They'd grown comfortable with moments of silence together because they each understood the creative mind and process. And then they would share where they drifted off to and give each other feedback.

She missed that. Emma smiled at him and nodded. Appreciated his support and encouragement once again. He understood her better than anyone.

Between Sheridan's wedding in a couple of weeks and the art show a month away, Emma fought the overwhelming feeling again. And she spent way more time with Manny these days than Calen, who always knew how to bring her back into a good place in her mind.

Maybe she needed to depend on her own ability to do that for herself instead of Calen. He had Nina now. And despite Manny's experience with his sister, he didn't seem to cue into the things that built up and caused anxiety for Emma.

Calen had a way of seeing it coming even before she did. She missed that, too. But she refused to let her neediness mess with his new relationship with Nina. They seemed pretty comfortable together. Not a lot of PDAs, but Calen had never been very comfortable with stuff like that. Even with her.

But she couldn't really recall seeing him serious about anyone now that she thought about it. She didn't have a clue what he was like with a girlfriend.

She followed Calen into the kitchenette. Manny stood by her two-seater dinette set and held the shirt Calen had given her up on his chest, chin down as he studied the design on the front. Then he flipped the shirt around and held it up to look at the back.

"I like the shirt you made, Calen, but I'm thinking if we're upscaling the event with my hors d'oeuvres, maybe we can enlist some of the wait staff from Madilyn's to carry trays as people mingle and view the artwork. What do you think?"

Calen shot her a glance before settling on Manny. Something hard settled behind his blank expression. "Yeah, whatever you think." He reached out and grabbed Nina's hand.

Nina gave him a quick look and then yawned. "Yep, it's official. The pumpkin is coming." She put her hand on Calen's chest and leaned against his shoulder. "Take me home, please?"

Calen leaned over a kissed the top of her head. "Sure thing."

So caring and sweet. That was Calen. Always thinking of others first. He'd only thought of her in planning the pre-show and now Manny, in his subtle way, was high-jacking it. But he meant well, didn't he?

Like Calen, he had her best interest at heart.

Didn't he?

Chapter Fourteen

As surreal as this day felt to Emma, she could only imagine how Sheridan must be feeling. She'd practically glowed in her dress during the fitting, but today...today she was the quintessential bride, radiating beauty at a whole new level.

And Noah...dressed in a traditional black tuxedo—cuz that's his style—he could give McSteamy Simon Basset from Bridgerton some serious competition. And watching her and Noah exchange vows had moved her to tears, but she fought to keep all eyes on the wedding couple.

Whenever the waterworks threatened, she glanced at either Manny, who didn't seem to notice her watery gazes—guess he was as captivated by the ceremony as she was—or Calen, who gave her a reassuring smile each time.

And Nina looked drop-dead gorgeous sitting next to him. They made such a cute couple. She couldn't remember seeing Calen in a suit before. Not recently anyway. When had his shoulders become so...broad?

Now that the happy couple had entered the reception

room, people mingled and waited for turns to extend their congratulations to the newlyweds.

Emma sat next to Manny at the wedding party table near the dance floor. She squeezed his hand. "Aren't they a gorgeous couple?"

Manny smiled at her and nodded. "Very."

Something seemed off with him. She leaned closer to ask if he was okay, but the sound of silverware clinking on a glass interrupted her.

Noah's father, looking rather dapper in his best man's tuxedo, stood, raising his glass. "To Mr. and Mrs. Kent."

Applause broke out in the room, punctuated by music as the band started to play their song. Hands linked, Noah and Sheridan made their way to the center of the dance floor.

Halfway into the song, Sheridan nodded at her. Her cue for Emma to bring Manny to the dance floor and encourage others to dance. With her father in prison, Sheridan had walked herself down the aisle alone, so she didn't want people wondering about a father-daughter dance.

"That's our cue." She rose and grabbed Manny's hand. As she walked onto the dance floor, she waved Calen and Nina over to join them. And Norman had enlisted Kaleena as his partner, and wow, did they look cute together. She made a mental note to ask Sheridan if something might be developing between those two.

"How cute is that?"

"What?" Manny's breath tickled her ear.

"Norman's dancing with Kaleena."

He lifted his head and glanced over his shoulder. "They look good together."

She clasped her hands behind his neck and tilted her head up. "Not as good as we do."

His slow smile tilted to one side. "Is that so?"

Emma nodded her head. "Very so." She searched his face for a moment for some sign or clue of what she'd sensed earlier. Though he returned her gaze, he seemed distracted. "Are you okay?"

What she really wanted to ask was, 'are we okay?' But that would sound too needy.

"I'm fine. Why do you ask?"

She lifted one shoulder. "I don't know. You just seem off."

He glanced away but said nothing.

Good thing she hadn't eaten, because her stomach clenched so hard she would have had to make a beeline to the planter by the edge of the dance floor to puke her guts out.

Tears burned her eyes. Funny how the ones that filled her eyes during the ceremony hadn't burned at all. "Manny, what is it? You can tell me anything, you know that, right? I love you."

"I know." He gave her a weak smile.

They continued to dance…why was he so quiet?

Her heart started to race, and her chest grew tight. No, no, no, she refused to have a panic attack in the middle of Sheridan's reception.

She closed her eyes and focused on her breathing. Deep inhale, slow exhale.

"Emma?"

She popped her eyes open.

Manny stared at her with a concerned expression. "Please don't get upset. I just didn't know how to tell you."

"Tell me what?" Her voice sounded panicked, even to herself. She searched for Calen's familiar face among the swaying couples surrounding them. Too many people. The music seemed louder too. She fought the urge to cry or run away. Or both.

She still couldn't locate Calen, so she focused on feeling her fingers and breathing.

"When I reached out to my contacts for your show, turns out one of them is opening a restaurant and he offered me the position as head chef."

"Where?" She spotted Calen dancing with Nina about twenty feet away.

"New York. I'm flying out tomorrow to look at the plans."

Emma tried to swallow, but her mouth felt full of sand. "Does Noah know?"

"Yes, of course. I told him right away. He encouraged me to check it out."

Noah already knew...and Manny had a flight booked already. That left one burning question. "How long have you known?"

He dragged his gaze upward. "A couple of weeks."

"Why did you wait to tell me?" She stared at his chest, remembering that day in her art studio when she sketched him, drew the line of his muscular neck to his sculpted shoulder, wondering what it would feel like to be held by him.

"Honestly, I wasn't sure what to tell you. I wasn't sure I wanted this, but the more I thought about it, the more I realized..."

"That you really do." Could she blame him? She gave him a tremulous smile. "I love you, Manny. How can I be anything but happy for you?"

"Really?"

"Yeah...of course." Her heart thumped hard, but at

least she could breathe. For the most part. "Can I ask you something?"

"Sure."

"If you take this job, have you thought about what that means for us?" Though fear of his answer gripped her so hard she struggled to breathe again, she gathered her waning courage and stared him straight in the face.

And there it was. The doubt sitting in his eyes was so heavy they appeared almost black.

"I don't know. I care about you very much."

"I thought you loved me?"

He'd told her he loved her, hadn't he?

"I said I was falling for you, Emma. I'm not even sure I'm ready for something more serious. And now, in light of this job offer... It's a brand new restaurant. I'll practically be living there night and day for at least the first six months."

In other words, he'd have no room in his life for a serious relationship.

For her.

She'd expected him to say they'd figure it out. That flights between Sarasota and New York were easy. Yet he talked about it as if it were a done deal. Now the distance she'd felt from him made complete sense. He was already on his way to New York and out of her life.

Her heart beat faster than the upbeat tempo of music the band had switched to. The panic attack sat right on the edge of winning its battle with her, but she kept fighting it back. "I understand."

She searched the room to get her bearings, tried to remember where the ladies' room door had been, looked for someplace to make an escape without drawing attention to herself.

The disco ball overhead spun and catapulted her back to that high school dance where her date dumped her on the dance floor. They say history repeats itself, but why did it have to make a reappearance today of all days?

She spotted the hallway leading to the restrooms and pushed away from Manny, but her heel caught on the hem of her dress, sending her backward.

Manny tried to reach for her, but something solid caught her from behind and then turned her around.

Calen pulled her against him. "I've got you, Emma."

Seeing Emma in distress had about done him in. He'd launched himself her way, leaving Nina standing there with just an 'Emma's in trouble' and a song half finished.

He barely made it in time to catch Emma, and now faced Manny's confused expression over her head. Calen clenched his jaw and sent him a look he hoped would convey the message of 'Get lost.' The last thing he wanted to do was punch the guy again.

Manny slid his hands into his trouser pockets, gave him a quick nod, and left the dance floor. He didn't head back to the wedding party table either. Instead, he kept walking and headed out the main doors of the reception room.

Emma had her head buried against his jacket lapel and her back shook against his hands as she sobbed against him.

He lowered his head, catching the sweet scent of her fragrance and the silky feel of her hair against his cheek. "It's gonna be okay."

She shook her head before leaning back to look up at him. Some of her makeup had smeared under her eyes. "No, it's not. He's leaving."

"Leaving?"

She sniffled as she swiped a hand across one cheek. "He got a job offer for a position as head chef at a new restaurant in New York."

"Oh...wow." He wanted the wipe the tears off of her other cheek. He wanted to hold her close and make the heartache he saw yet again in her eyes go away. He wanted to kiss her despite the slobbery mess she was.

"Yeah...wow." She sniffled again and wiped her other cheek.

But what did that mean? Were she and Manny over, or just dealing with a hiccup in their relationship? Because he knew Emma. Knew that when she loved someone, she didn't hold back. And he could see her picking up her life and moving to New York to be with Manny.

"Will you...will you go with him?" He couldn't breathe, just waited for her to answer.

Emma's tears had stopped, and her expression hardened. "The only thing Manny is sure he wants right now is to be a head chef, and this is a once-in-a-lifetime opportunity."

Her sarcastic tone didn't hide the hurt one bit.

"I'm so sorry, Emma."

She gave him a forced smile. "No big deal. At least now I know where I stand with him. Bottom of the list, as usual." Her eyes darted back and forth as she searched his face. Her lips trembled. "Why, Calen? Why doesn't anyone want to fall in love with me?"

Her words were like a gut punch and sucked the air from him, which was probably a good thing because it kept him from blurting out how he really felt. Because right now the temptation to say, *I want you, Emma. I'm in love with you and it seems I always have been,* had never been stronger.

So he said it the only way he could at the moment. He snickered and threw his hands to his sides. "Hey now, you know you always have me."

She gave his sarcasm a half-hearted laugh. "I know."

He folded her into his arms again, hurting for her more than he could ever recall and loving her so much that he felt the overwhelming ache of wanting her in every cell of his being.

As the band finished the song, they shifted into a familiar tune. The vocalist stepped up to the mic and began to sing the lyrics to 'You're My Satellite.'

Standing near the stage, Nina smiled and waved at him as she pointed to the band. She'd set him up again. Calen shook his head and gave her a smile of thanks.

Not that Emma would notice in her current state of mind—

"Hey, they're playing our song." Emma pulled back, a glimmer of a smile on her face. A good sign…maybe.

He grinned down at her. Even with makeup smeared under her eyes, she was adorable. "Yeah, our song."

"I'm sorry I'm taking you away from Nina. There I go, being selfish again." Tears pooled in the bottom of her eyes again.

"It's not a problem. Trust me."

"What do you mean?"

He sighed. "Nina and I are just friends, Emma."

"I thought you two were getting close?"

"We're friends. That's all."

"I'm sorry it didn't work out." She wore her heart on her face on that one.

What did he say? Me too? In a way, he was, but in all truth, not really. Nina was great, but his heart was too tangled up with Emma.

She snuggled back against him as they swayed to the tune. At first, he hesitated to hold her—really hold her—but then his arms seemed to have a mind of their own and tightened his hold on her. One hand splayed against her lower back while the other went for her hair. He brushed the long tendrils she left dangling out from her face before resting his hand on her upper back. Without thinking, he lowered his head and kissed the top of hers.

Emma snapped her head up to look at him, but she said nothing. Just studied him with those blue eyes that invited him to drown in their depths. Then she blinked and laid her head against his chest, just under his chin.

He hadn't meant to do that, but he didn't regret it either. Emma probably thought it was just his way of comforting her, which it was.

But if she only knew…

Wadsworth's 'I Wandered Lonely as a Cloud' took on a new meaning for him as the song continued. Emma was his 'dance with the daffodils' and always would be.

Chapter Fifteen

Emma seemed oddly calm for the rest of the dance to "their song." Once it ended, she had kissed him on the cheek and thanked him, just like she had all those years ago at the high school when that shlep of a boyfriend dumped her during the dance.

Like what Manny had done. Only he hadn't really dumped Emma. He'd chosen something more important to him, which still amounted to Emma feeling the sting of rejection and him wanting to introduce the guy to his fist again.

After that, she'd walked away slowly toward the restrooms, saying she needed to clean her face up for the rest of reception. She had maid of honor duties to fulfill.

He returned to the table assigned to him and Nina and dropped into his chair in a blind daze. Good thing tomorrow was his day off because Emma would need at least a full day of Mr. Bean to begin her recovery over this one. Perhaps more...

Calen could understand Manny's position to some

degree, but regarding Emma, he couldn't understand how anything could be more important than her. But his head and heart were now in cahoots together and had turned him into a lovesick idiot.

Nina plopped into the chair next to him. "That looked intense."

He glanced at her but kept his chin down. "You can say that again."

"Okay, that looked intense." She leaned over to give him a full view of her expression that screamed 'details, please.'

"Manny broke her heart."

"He dumped her?"

"Kind of."

Nina frowned. "Kind of? How do you kind of dump someone?"

"He got a job offer in New York."

She sat back. "Ah, I see. He doesn't want her to come with him?"

"I guess not. She said he doesn't want a serious relationship right now."

"Ouch…yeah, that's rough."

He put his elbows on his knees and held his head. "I'm really not sure what to do here."

Nina put her hand on his back. "Just be her friend, like usual. The last thing she needs right now is more complications."

With a groaning sigh, he sat back. "Agreed."

Emma came into view as she made her way to where Sheridan stood chatting with some wedding attendees. Even from a distance, he could tell she forced a smile.

Nina grabbed his hand. "How about a dance?"

He squeezed her hand as he formulated his words. "I told Emma the truth. That you and I are just friends." He darted his gaze to where Emma stood with her back to them.

Nina followed his line of sight. "I get it."

"Thank you for trying to help things along."

Nina leaned in to kiss him. She didn't linger, just a tender kiss.

This didn't feel like her usual fake-girlfriend performance. "Why did you do that?"

"Because you're a great guy, Calen. Probably for the best that we stop this charade now." She laughed as she stood. "A girl could really fall for a guy like you."

The undercurrent of her reply brought his full attention.

Her eyes turned glassy, which made his gut clench. The last thing he ever wanted was for Nina to get hurt. "I'm sorry, Nina."

"No worries. If you don't mind, I'm going to head home."

He checked on Emma's whereabouts and found her on the dance floor with Noah's dad. She'd pulled herself together better than he expected.

"I can drive you." He rose from his seat.

"No, you should stay for Emma. I can find my way home." She grabbed her purse from the table and paused. "I hope she realizes how special you are."

He didn't say anything—didn't know what to say— before she turned away. Why couldn't he have fallen for Nina instead? They made sense together. Shared a love for poetry and tea. And based on what she implied, she would have been more than interested in pursuing a relationship.

Though extravagant, the food tables didn't hold any appeal at the moment. He slid back into his seat to keep an eye on Emma, like a watchdog waiting for his owner to come home.

If only she knew how fully she owned his heart.

Dancing with Norman gave Emma a chance to regroup, and she was pretty sure that was why he asked her to dance. The man had a heart of gold and he knew his way around a paintbrush, too.

"Thank you, Norman."

Though not as tall as his son, Norman still had a couple of inches on her. "For what? I saw a pretty girl who needed a dance partner and stepped in."

She'd grown to love having Norman in her art classes. He always knew how to encourage people and did it regularly in her classes. "You're such a sweetheart." Her voice cracked with her emotions. She felt like a wrung-out rag bleached out by the sun. "Sorry. An emotional day."

Norman nodded. "I noticed Manny left."

She dropped her gaze and took a deep breath. "He had to leave early."

"I know it's none of my business, but you seemed pretty upset. I'm glad Calen was there to back you up."

A soft laugh preceded her words. "Calen's always there." She checked Calen's table to find Calen sitting alone.

"I chatted with him after your class that day. He's a really great guy."

"Who, Manny?"

"No, Calen. He seems to really care about you."

Why was Norman talking about Calen instead of Manny?

"We've been best friends for years. He always has my back and I have his."

"What if he wanted your front, too?" He chuckled.

Emma blinked twice. "What do you mean?"

Norman shrugged and smiled, reminding her of Noah. "Nothing. Just wondered if there might be something more there between you two."

She shifted her gaze again to where Calen sat, leaning forward in his chair and watching her. He'd kissed her on her head, like she'd seen him do with Nina. At the time, it kind of shocked her and made her wonder if he might feel something for her, but she'd brushed it off as a déjà vu moment of when he danced with her in high school after her boyfriend dumped her.

After that night, she'd wondered if Calen had developed feelings for her, but he never said or did anything to confirm that impression. Now it just seemed his way of showing he cared about her when she wound up rejected yet again by another loser.

"No, just best friends. Calen's kind of my rock."

The band kept the music slow as they switched to another song, so when Norman continued to dance, she went along, enjoying the peace of his presence.

"My Madilyn was my rock. My best friend in the entire world."

"You two were together a long time, weren't you?"

"Almost forty years. But we started out as friends."

"You did?" Why did it seem like Norman had a point here?

"Yes, for a couple of years. I thought she'd keep me in the friend zone forever until one day, she didn't."

"What changed?" As she waited for Norman to answer, she tracked Calen's movements to the food table, which he passed by as he made his way to talk to the woman who owned the Sass & Sun. Emma remembered her only because Calen mentioned Kaleena wanted to put copies of his poetry book in her store. She'd loved the woman right away for that.

"I don't know. I guess something shifted in her mind and one day she looked at me differently. That's what she told me, anyway."

She could understand someone changing their mind, but what about the heart? Especially when hers was still so entangled with Manny.

Could she do that with Calen—see him differently? Maybe she already was because she was relieved when Calen told her he and Nina were just friends. Granted, she'd acknowledged a smidge of jealousy over Nina's presence in Calen's life, but she'd amounted that to just being possessive of her best friend.

Could it be more?

Calen had held a very special place in her life for years. He'd been there for her when no one else could really understand what she was going through. Even her parents hadn't fully understood her anxiety attacks or how to help her. They'd resorted to calling Calen for help when she experienced bad ones because he was the only one who could talk her down.

Not that he said much, just told her to breathe and focus on him. Which she did, stared into his hazel eyes as her heartbeat returned to normal and the pressure in her chest released. Later on, she'd learned to close her eyes and just picture him if they weren't together, like he'd trained her. Kind of reminded her of Pavlov's dog.

"You must miss Madilyn a lot, Norman."

"Terribly." He didn't hesitate in his answer, and his

expression turned serious. "I miss my wife, don't get me wrong. But I think I miss my best friend more."

Tears burned her eyes again. She blinked them back as she tore her gaze away from Norman and instinctively looked for Calen.

And there he sat, still watching her. Her best friend who did life with her in so many ways.

Had the right guy for her been there all along and she'd missed it?

Chapter Sixteen

Emma finished loading the dishwasher and switched it on. The week before Sheridan's wedding had been packed with last-minute details needing her attention and her tiny apartment had reflected the neglect. While her best friend—who was a girl—went on a honeymoon in Paris with her new husband, she'd spent the morning cleaning and restoring order.

For certain, a better choice than sitting around and moping over Manny. He'd sent her an 'I'm sorry' in a text this morning, but she hadn't bothered to reply. Everything was so confusing—she didn't know what to say. Didn't know what to feel. Didn't know what she wanted, if she were to be perfectly honest with herself.

All she knew was that something felt different about this breakup. Yes, Manny's decision hurt, but not as much as she thought it would. Maybe she still held hope that he'd change his mind and realize he didn't want to leave. Or maybe he'd even ask her to go with him. And they'd live happily ever after.

But did she really want that? Did she love him enough to change her life so drastically? And if she could ask herself that, how could she fault Manny for being honest with her about what he wanted?

She growled as she tossed the kitchen towel onto the counter. Too many questions swirled in her head, leaving her exhausted. And it wasn't even lunchtime. At least her apartment was clean now.

A soft knock came from her front door. She barely had it open before Calen whooshed in carrying a grocery sack.

He went into her kitchen, dropped the bag on the counter, and pulled out the contents one by one. "I bought the usual. Buttered popcorn and Snow-Caps to mix *with* the popcorn. And a large bottle of Diet Coke, which just seems to be the biggest contradiction in this scenario."

Here he stood again, ready to help shovel her heart back into her chest and get a grip on her life. "I didn't know you were coming."

His expression turned baffled as he leaned against the counter. "Don't I always?"

"Yeah, you do. Kind of selfish of me, don't you think?"

"What do you mean? This is what we do, right?"

"Yeah, we do, but I think I'm done with it." Her heart needed a break.

"Done with Mr. Bean? Is there such a thing?" His sarcasm made her smile, which was why he did it.

"I'm fine, Calen. Seriously. Mr. Bean doesn't have to make an appearance this time."

"Wow, didn't see that coming." His voice deepened, almost guttural with emotion. "What can I do then?"

Something different drew her to him. Not the usual comfortable friendship they'd shared for years. Something deeper... "Nothing, I guess. I don't know. I'm not sure what I want anymore."

The way he stared at her, as if he saw into the depths of her soul, brought home *the something*. Calen saw her, really saw her. Flaws and all. Didn't matter the circumstances or what he may have going on in his own life, he always showed up, determined to help her, save her, and protect her.

How had she not seen him before this? The way his eyes softened when he looked at her. The way his smile tilted up on one side when he had a quippy line to share. The way he always seemed to be there when she needed someone or something.

Even if it was just a hair band that he carried in his wallet...

He hadn't shaved and, with the way his hair fell forward, gave him a rugged look. And he certainly had filled out that suit at the wedding yesterday. She'd grown so comfortable with Calen as her best friend that she'd neglected to see him as Calen the man, too.

The man who caught her on the dance floor yesterday...

Step by intentional step, she closed the distance between them until she was close enough to hold his arms, lift up onto the balls of her feet, and touch her lips to his. And not just a peck. She wanted to know what it felt like to kiss him.

And to really be kissed by Calen Cooper.

Like she'd seen him kiss Nina. Like she's wondered while they'd danced together. And like she'd imagined all morning as she cleaned her apartment instead of crying over Manny.

Telling...

He stiffened at first, but then his arms slid around her. Pulled her against him. Held her. He leaned into the kiss, taking the lead as he fanned one hand against the small of her back and cupped the side of her face with the other.

And just as she thought this might turn into the kiss she'd imagined, he pulled back.

His gaze was intense and dark, while his breathing sounded rough. "Emma, what are you doing?"

Emma ran her hand over the stubble on his cheek, sending a wave of longing and desire through him that threatened his decision to step back and make sure she wasn't just reacting to her breakup with Manny.

"Kissing you, or so I thought." She blinked at him. Sunlight from the kitchen window made her blue eyes appear ethereal.

He wanted nothing more than to kiss her again, to give into that ache that had stayed silent for too long and now demanded to be heard, but if Emma really wanted to pursue this, he'd make sure it was for the right reason.

"This isn't a good idea." He relaxed his arms and dropped them to his sides, missing the way she felt immediately.

"Why?" Her eyes did little bounces back and forth as she studied him.

Could she see how much she affected him? He dropped his gaze. "Because it's just a rebound thing."

She lowered her hand. "Not as much as you might think."

Her reply caught him by surprise. He'd come expecting

to find her red-eyed and weepy with a growing mountain of used tissues on the coffee table. "What?"

Her whole demeanor shifted as she closed herself off. Just like she did in high school when the subject of her father came up. "Never mind."

As she turned away, he grabbed her arm. "Explain."

He must have sounded firmer than he intended because she startled, so he softened his tone. "Please."

"Why? So you can analyze it with your wit and rhetoric?"

This time he jerked back as he released her wrist. "What does that mean?"

"You always dance around your feelings, Calen. Are you passionate about anything?"

Was she lashing out at him because she was mad at Manny, or did she regret kissing him and realize she'd made a mistake?

Taking a page from his own book, he clenched his jaw as he breathed deeply through his nose, then exhaled through his mouth. The last thing he wanted to do was react and regret. Words spoken without forethought led down a dangerous path of no return.

"I'm sorry, Calen. I didn't mean that—"

If he didn't leave now, he'd do something he'd regret. He just didn't know what at this point. "Enjoy your Mr. Bean fest. Tell him I said hello."

Calen strode out of the kitchen but paused at her front door. Maybe there was one thing that needed to be said, and maybe it was time she heard it. Because if they were ever to have a chance at something more than friendship, he had to make sure he didn't wind up on her list of messy breakups.

"I understand you're hurting, Emma. And you've been hurt by a lot of guys. But until you deal with the pain your real father caused you, you won't find what you're looking for."

Chapter Seventeen

She stood there, stunned by his words. As the door shut, she grabbed the box of Sno-Caps from the counter and hurled it at the door. The box rattled when it made contact, then slid to the floor.

How could he say something like that to her?

He knew how she felt about the subject of her real father. Why would he toss that in her face at such a low point of her life?

What kind of friend did that?

Emma flopped onto the couch with a box of tissues, unable to hold back the waterworks. She couldn't call Sheridan and no way would she call her mother. She'd probably agree with Calen.

She blew her nose and tossed the tissue onto the coffee table. Calen had to be wrong. She pushed off the couch and went into her bedroom. The sand dollar Manny had given her still sat on her dresser, too delicate to go into her memory box.

With that thought in mind, she got down on the floor

and pulled her memory box out from under her bed. Why not walk down memory lane and see the other failed bits of her life?

Emma lifted the lid and pushed it back against the foot of her bed. Various pieces of memorabilia lay stacked in disarray in the container. She pushed aside several items to unearth the one photo album she had from her early childhood.

Her mother had only kept it for Emma and gave it to her when she graduated high school. She hadn't looked at the photos since then. The binding had cracked, but the photo sleeves were still in good shape. She flipped past the first pages of her as an infant to get to the last images of her with her birth father.

As she scanned the pictures, the reality that most of the men she'd dated had the same dark hair and eyes as her father sank in. Was that what Calen was implying? That she dated guys that looked like her father because she was trying to fix the pain he'd caused her?

The last picture of her with her father was after her parents had divorced and the last time she ever saw him. They stood in front of the Bush Gardens sign at the entrance. She didn't remember much from that day, only that they'd had to leave early because Emma had a panic attack on a ride.

After that trip, he never even called her again. She figured he'd had enough of his defective daughter and moved on.

She dropped the album into the container and grabbed her phone.

Her mother's voice brought a fresh wave of tears. "Emma, are you okay?"

She took a deep breath. "No, not really. I think things are over for Manny and me."

"Oh honey, I'm so sorry. I know how happy you've been. What happened?"

"He got a job offer in New York. It's a really great opportunity for him." She grabbed another tissue to wipe her face and nose.

"I see. Well, sometimes that happens. Maybe you two can have a long-distance relationship for a while."

"No, he doesn't want that kind of commitment right now."

"What about you, Emma? What do you want?"

She sighed. "I don't know, to be honest. I thought I really loved him, but now I'm not so sure."

Her dad's voice filtered over the line. "Is that Emma?"

Her mother's voice grew faint as she answered her dad's question and filled him in. "Your dad says hello and that maybe Calen should punch some sense into the guy."

Emma giggled with her mother. "No need. It's probably for the best."

"That's my girl. There's always a bright side to everything, right?"

She loved her mother's eternal optimism. If she were an animal, she'd be a dolphin.

"Mom, can I ask you a question about my father? My birth father, I mean."

"Uh...sure." Her mother sounded wary.

"Did he not love me at all?"

"Oh, sweetheart, of course he did."

"Then why did he just disappear after that trip to Bush Gardens?"

Her mother sighed. "I think he blamed himself for your anxiety issues."

"Why would he blame himself?" She flipped open the album to look at another picture of him holding her as a baby.

"Your attacks always seemed to hit when you were with him. I think he thought you'd be happier without him."

"That's awful."

"I know, sweetheart. But no one's perfect, you know? He did what he thought was best for you."

She started crying again, thinking about her father making that kind of sacrifice. "So it wasn't because he couldn't stand to be around me?"

"Oh, heavens no, Emma. Not at all. I just think he felt like he did more harm than good in your life. I tried to tell him otherwise, but I think he felt you would be better off with Bob as your father. That's why he asked Bob to adopt you."

"He wanted that?"

"We all did, sweetheart. I know it was difficult for you, and I didn't tell you that part because I didn't want you to think your father didn't want you. He did, he just felt you'd be better off without him. He never thought much of himself. I think that was a big part of his problem in life, to be honest."

Wow. She had no idea her birth father had felt like that. All this time Emma thought it was she who could never measure up to his expectations when, in reality, he was the one who thought he couldn't measure up and be a good father.

"Honey, are you okay? I would have told you sooner if I'd known you were struggling with this."

"No, it's okay. I didn't realize I needed to hear it, to be honest."

"What brought this on, if you don't mind me asking?"

"Oh, just something Calen said." She'd thank him for it after she quit being mad at him for being right.

"He's such a great guy, Emma. You know we love him like a son already."

What was her mother implying? "Thanks, Mom. I love you. Tell Dad I love him too."

"I will."

After saying goodbye, Emma looked through the album once more. Looking at the pictures didn't strangle her heart anymore. Now that she had a better understanding, she studied the image of her father from a different perspective.

She still wished he had tried a little harder to be in her life, but at least now she knew her issues hadn't pushed him away. He'd made that decision on his own.

And she didn't have to feel responsible for it anymore.

As he drove home, the stunned look on Emma's face haunted him. Had he made a mistake telling her that? He mentally shook himself. Didn't matter now. No undo button for poor decisions existed, no matter how hard he wished for one.

And Emma's words pounded in his mind like a sledge-hammer. What did she mean when she asked what was he passionate about? He was passionate about his poetry. She knew that and had encouraged him to submit his work.

And the coffee shop came from that, his idealistic view of who he wanted to be as a poet. Yes, even a romantic sometimes, but that's how he rolled. And he'd gotten good at rolling with the punches when it came to Emma. Maybe too good.

He shouldn't have left. Should have stayed and talked

things out. For all he knew, she could be having a full-blown panic attack over what just happened between them. But then again, maybe not. She seemed calmer than he expected—not the blubbering mess that she usually would be the day after, sitting on her couch, binging episodes of Mr. Bean.

Maybe mentioning her father hadn't been a bad idea. If she'd figured out how to deal with the situation without his help, maybe she didn't need him anymore...what if her time with Manny had helped her resolve some of those issues she'd had regarding her father and now emotionally, she'd moved on? He couldn't help but applaud her for that.

But passionless? Did she really not know him? Or had he hidden his feelings for her for so long that he had inadvertently hidden himself as well?

Once home, he stomped into his apartment and flopped onto his couch. The bookshelves behind his television held mostly poetry books, as well as novels and magazines. But the cabinet on the right side concealed his journals—years of poetic writings and outpourings.

He crouched in front of the open cabinet, pulling out book after book of his most intimate thoughts and ponderings. Compositions that held rhymes, iambic pentameter, haikus, limericks, sonnets, and even some song lyrics. On the pages, he felt free to express his deepest feelings.

Not so much in life though. He'd learned early on to shield that part of himself from a world that didn't understand his sensitivities.

But he had to ask himself again. Had he hidden himself so well that Emma never saw him?

One way to fix that. He flipped through several of his journals and grabbed a stack of the most detailed ones. He'd prove to Emma he was as far from passionless as the sun was from the earth, and even then more so. The earth still felt the heat of the sun.

He rushed out of his apartment, ignoring the small voice that tried to talk him out of doing such a brazen act of vulnerability. Once and for all, he'd settle this thing between him and Emma. He would take the necessary steps instead of waiting around.

Maybe then he would get some closure and get on with his life, either with Emma...

Or without.

The thought stopped him as he got in his car and stayed his hand from starting the engine.

Could he live a life devoid of Emma?

Maybe the bigger question he needed to settle was, could he continue their friendship considering the feelings he clearly still had for her?

That pushed him forward all the way back to her place. Once parked, he grabbed the journals and strode up the walk to her door without even closing his car door.

He pushed the bell multiple times. No turning back now.

Her door flew open and there she stood, a puzzled expression on her face. Her eyes were red from crying and her eyelashes still appeared moist.

"Calen." She sounded breathy...surprised.

He faltered for a moment—doubted his course of action, but seeing her just confirmed his need for resolution. A life spent pining for someone he couldn't have wasn't a life well lived. He didn't know who said that originally—didn't care either. He just knew he had to do this.

Calen thrust the journals at her. "Here. This should prove I'm not passionless."

She called after him as he strode back down the sidewalk to his car, but he didn't stop or turn around. Just got in his car and drove away.

Because seeing her there like that, and knowing he caused those tears gutted him. Didn't matter that he might be in love with Emma—he couldn't stand the thought of hurting her.

Might be in love? Who was he kidding? Being Emma's best friend had been his consolation prize when he was seventeen. But that kiss woke up every dormant feeling he ever had for Emma and set ablaze a fiery ache for her he'd never felt before; as if his heart had just been waiting for the right accelerant.

He drove toward his shop, parked, and headed toward the back door, but changed direction to Kaleena's place. When he reached the door to Sass & Sun, he went in and waited, unsure if he could even talk about the mess in his head at the moment.

Kaleen's smile slipped as she looked up from the register. "Okay, who died?"

He didn't say a word, just brushed past her and made a more definitive path to the changing room. Then he stood there, staring at the oversized, quilted, olive green ottoman. Could he talk about it? Really talk about it?

If he didn't, he might do something stupid, like confess to Emma that he didn't think they could be friends anymore. Then she'd ask why and he'd have to tell her.

Because I think I'm in love with you. That I may have always been in love with you...

Yeah, that would go over like the sludge in a day-old pot of coffee. And just as boring. Not passionate like Manny. He dropped to the ottoman and held his head in his hands.

Kaleena didn't say a word. Just sat down next to him and put her hand on his shoulder.

Almost sounded like she was talking at one point, barely a whisper. Probably praying. She said she prayed. Maybe she could ask God to fix him.

Because he needed fixing really bad.

She sighed. "Whenever you're ready."

He nodded. Tried to speak, but the pain in his heart radiated into his chest and knotted the muscles in his throat. Perhaps some things needed to be left unsaid.

Besides, what would it accomplish? He and Emma would never be anything but friends. The problem, though, was he didn't think he could go back to the friend zone. Not this time.

Not after that kiss. Not after knowing how she felt in his arms. And certainly not after he'd just bared his soul to her by giving her his most recent journals.

What was he thinking?

But he needed to know for sure—needed to know what he was feeling wasn't just a crush but the full-blown, real deal. "What does true love look like?"

Kaleena pursed her lips as she thought. "Lots of ways, really. Depends. But, I can tell you this. If you find yourself willing to sacrifice your own happiness for the sake of another person, then you're probably in love. Big time."

He dropped his hands between his knees and nodded. "Then I think I'm in trouble."

"Emma?"

Calen nodded again.

"Have you told her how you feel?"

"No." Eyes closed, he dropped his head back.

"Why not?"

"Because I haven't figured things out yet. And besides, she's still in love with Manny."

"But Sheridan mentioned they broke up."

"Seems that way." He ran his hands over his face.

"So maybe it's time you told her." Kaleena tilted her head to look at him.

Emma's shocked expression replayed in his head. Hadn't he told Emma enough already? "I don't think I can."

"Okay, at the risk of sounding like a broken record, why not?"

"Because she doesn't see me that way." Although she did initiate that kiss. What if he was wrong?

"Maybe she just needs some time to get over Manny, and then she'll realize you are the right guy for her."

He swiveled his head to look at Kaleena. "You think I'm the right guy for her?"

"Well, duh, have you met you yet? You're an amazing guy, Calen. She'd be crazy to pick anyone else."

He dropped his head into his hands. Could Kaleena be right?

Regardless of what Emma decided about him, he knew how pathetic he was. How much of a goner he was. How irrevocably in love he was with his best friend.

Because no matter what—or who—she chose, she would always be the brightest star in his galaxy.

Chapter Eighteen

How had her life gone from sucky to super-sized sucky? First, she lost Manny and now she may have lost her lifelong best friend.

At least she settled the issue about her birth father. Her mother would be so proud of her optimism right now.

Emma clutched a pillow to her chest and curled into a ball on her couch. The remote sat next to the stack of Calen's journals.

Mr. Bean or Calen Cooper?

She reached for the remote and turned on the TV, then clicked on a random episode of Mr. Bean. But his quirky grunts and goofy antics did little for her this time. She glanced at Calen's journals again. How could she accuse him of being passionless? How could a poet be passionless?

Emma closed her eyes and pictured Calen's face, his hazel eyes with those speckles of olive green, his endearing smile that tilted to one side when he had planned a zinger and had waited all day to spring it on her.

She kept replaying that moment in her head when she

opened the door. She'd wanted to hug him, tell him she was sorry again, that she shouldn't have said what she did. But though her easy-going Calen still lurked in there some-where, the sternness of his expression had stopped her in her tracks. She's pushed too hard and felt like the biggest turd for it too. Never in her life had she felt so alone.

She muted the TV and grabbed a journal from the top of the stack. Read the first page, flipped to the next, and then the next, pausing at points as his words twined into her chest and grabbed hold of her heart. She didn't know how much time had passed until she noticed the sun no longer shone through her living room window and her stomach growled.

All but two of Calen's journals lay in an array around her on the couch. She thought she knew Calen, really knew him. But this? His journals painted a side of him she'd only glimpsed on rare occasions. Yeah, she teased him about his word studies, how he made his dictionary app part of his daily reading, and how he'd insert his researched words into a conversation to test them out—all of that she knew was part of his passion for poetry.

But reading his journals was like stepping into an inti-macy with him she'd never experienced. His passion for life overflowed on the pages and he had an amazing way of expressing the simplest of moments in a way that made them profound. His words flowed with deep symbolism that left her awestruck as she comprehended the depth of his perceptions and meanings.

She encountered his heart in his words in a way she never had before and his words moved her. Deeply. To say Calen was a man of few words could only apply to his verbal language because he was a vault of unlimited expres-sion on the page.

Especially about stars, the moon, and the sun. Did he have a fascination with space that he'd never shared with her?

Emma didn't know what to think about him anymore. That night she'd massaged his neck while he sat on her front step flooded back. The way he looked up at her—she'd brushed that moment off because she'd been so enamored with Manny. And what about the evening he came to her studio with the shirt he designed, excited about his plan to help her work get more attention even before the show?

And the ponytail holder in his wallet—so simple yet so profound...

That and so many other things he'd done just for her, that she'd accepted as part of their friendship...what if Calen had been telling her he cared—no, loved her all along?

She thought she loved Manny; had told him many times, but as she recalled their moments together, she couldn't remember him saying it back to her. Not directly.

He's said he was falling for her that evening in her studio. She's assumed he meant he loved her. And after that, anytime she told him again, he either said 'I know' or would kiss her. Which again, she'd taken to mean he loved her too.

But did he? Really love her?

Could Calen really love her like that? They'd been best friends for so long...and he'd always been the one to catch her when life knocked her down.

Like when he caught her at the reception. He didn't just catch her fall physically. Calen had caught her emotionally, too. Always had.

Her phone pinged on the coffee table. She picked it up, expecting to see a text from Calen. But it was Manny...

I fly back tomorrow, and I really need to talk to you, Emma.

She resisted the urge to throw her phone at Mr. Bean's silent figure on the television, but the moving dots indicated he was still typing.

His next text left her breathless.

I love you.

Calen had slept very little through the night, mostly tossed and turned until he gave up, showered, and headed to the coffee shop early. He cleaned the coffee and espresso machines and defrosted the mini fridge in his office, all while refusing to let his mind fill with thoughts of Emma and wondering if she'd read any of his journals yet. He'd tried so hard not to react to her words, but handing off his poetry to her like that had been exactly that—pure reaction.

And now his rash actions left him feeling exposed and vulnerable.

No point in agonizing over it now. Really would be nice if life had an undo button.

When Steph arrived and surveyed the place, she'd raised her brows but didn't say a word. Which was good, because he was in no mood to talk. Or even write. He'd tried many times during the night to relieve the churning chaos in his head and heart; but to no avail.

He felt like Romeo, trapped in a world of his own longings and forbidden to express them.

What did he do next? Apologize to Emma? Try to restore their friendship? Some things just couldn't be undone and other things couldn't go back to normal. He feared their friendship could be one of those things, but he had to at least try, right?

He finished restocking the cups and napkins behind the

counter and rose, stretching his back. Movement across the street captured his attention. Manny, to be exact. He opened the door to Madilyn's and went inside.

Calen shot from behind the counter. "Watch the shop."

Steph's clear understanding followed him out the glass door. "Oh, boy."

He didn't stop, strode across the street like a soldier on a mission. His heart slammed in his chest and his shoulders tensed. No matter what happened with him and Emma, he'd make sure Manny had a clear picture of her best interests.

Once inside, he scanned the restaurant until he found Manny talking to the bartender. Manny did a sort of double take when he saw Calen, then walked toward him.

"Hi, Calen. What brings you in?" Manny appeared tired.

Had he just flown back from New York? And how much longer would he be in town? Emma made it sound like the interview was just a formality.

"Can we talk?"

Manny's expression turned skeptical. "Just talk?"

Calen closed his eyes and suppressed a groan. "No punching, if that's what you're asking."

"Sure, we can use Noah's office." Manny led him to the back, to a smallish office with two desks.

Once he closed the door, Manny leaned against one desk and crossed his arms. "I assume this is about Emma?"

Calen rubbed the back of his neck, then nodded. "Are you taking the job in New York?"

"That's really none of your business, but since you asked, I haven't decided yet."

He paused, waiting for Manny to say more and considering his next line of verbal attack. A person could use words as effectively as fists. "I'm concerned for Emma."

"I know you are, but I'm also wondering if there isn't something more to that concern. Is there, Calen?" Manny tilted his head as he studied him.

"Like you say, none of your business. I just want to make sure you don't hurt her more than you already have."

Manny dropped his arms and pinched the bridge of his nose. "You're a good friend, Calen." When he lifted his head, he appeared sad. "I haven't accepted the job yet because I realized I'm in love with Emma. Being back in New York wasn't as great as I'd expected. All I could think about was her."

His eyes pleaded for understanding while Calen's gut did a full nose dive into the dark abyss of unrequited love, as the poets loved to quote. Yet he had no desire to romanticize.

Emma would be ecstatic. She'd finally have what she always wanted. He would bow out and return to the friend zone. If he could. He'd at least try for her sake. And succeed for a while as she and Manny spent a lot of time together, renewing their relationship. Meanwhile, Calen would fade into the background of her life and figure out how to move on with his.

"Have you seen her yet? Does she know?"

Manny shook his head. "Not yet. I'm going to her place after I close up the place tonight so we can talk."

That's right. Noah and Sheridan were on their honeymoon, so Manny must be stepping in to help manage the place in their absence.

He swallowed down the growing knot in his throat. "Don't break her heart again, Manny."

Manny's expression turned earnest. "I never intended to

hurt her, Calen. Just took me a minute to realize I'm in love with her."

That's what he needed to know. Manny loved Emma. He could walk away, knowing they at least had a shot at something good, despite it being the most painful thing he'd ever done in his life.

But he would do it for her.

Calen held his hand out to Manny. "No hard feelings?"

Manny shook his hand, then gave him a tight smile. "Not at all. I know you're just looking out for her. Being a good *friend*."

Calen didn't miss the emphasis Manny put on that last word. Point made. He nodded and then left as quick as his feet could carry himself without going into a full jog. The shake had felt like a passing of the guard; like he'd turned over all that concerned him about Emma over to Manny.

In a way, he felt less burdened, but that did little at the moment to relieve the brick his heart had turned into.

He needed time. That's all. He'd throw himself into his shop and finally put together those poetry submissions.

And learn to change his orbit since Emma would no longer be his sun.

Chapter Nineteen

Emma worked on one of her pieces for the art show while she waited for Manny to show up. This time she didn't bother with candles or staging a romantic setting. She'd done that before only to painfully realize that their love was one-sided. Saying I love you in a text was one thing. Saying it to the intended person face to face was another. No more rose-colored glasses.

Calen would call her analogy cliché, but she thought it appropriate.

Her heart caught on her thoughts. She hadn't spoken to Calen—not even a text—in almost three days, which felt like forever. Normally they texted each other every day to at least say hello, how are you, or whatever.

But not for lack of trying. At least on her part. She'd picked up her phone so many times to text Calen, but for the life of her, couldn't think of what to say. How did they bounce back to a friendship after what she did?

And the things they said to each other…that alone made her want to hide from Calen, which felt so weird.

He'd always been the one she ran to, and he'd always been there for her.

After she straightened things out with Manny tonight, she'd have a clearer head to talk to Calen. She'd go see him tomorrow and try to fix things with him. Hopefully, he'd forgive her and they could be friends of some sort.

Maybe not as close as they used to be, but something... she couldn't imagine her life without Calen. At all.

And oddly, she was having a hard time imagining a future with Manny. Maybe that would change once she saw him and heard him tell her in person that he loved her. The real deal this time.

She dabbed her brush into the last bit of her Prussian blue and touched her brush to the wash she'd created to add more depth to the background. This painting captured an area on Five Points, where five downtown streets converged and where the Pineapple Drop happened every New Year's Eve.

"That's amazing." Manny's voice startled her from behind.

At least this time, she'd leaned back in time not to smudge her painting.

"Hi." She swished the brush in her water cup, squeegeed the bristle with her fingers, and stuck the brush in her bun. She really should start setting up her easel so she faced the door.

She swiveled on her stool to stare at Manny—she needed a moment to assess her heart and mind before jumping in again.

He lingered in the doorway to her studio, looking worn. His smile even seemed tired. Had he changed his mind? Did he have doubts?

Did she?

She slowly rose from her seat as he moved toward her. "Welcome back."

Funny...she'd imagined this moment, pictured herself running into his arms and kissing him as he professed his love for her. Instead, her shoes felt stuck to the floor.

Something inside held her back.

"I missed you, Emma." He linked his fingers with one of her hands.

She nodded and tried to smile. "How was your trip?"

"Awful."

She frowned. "Didn't things work out?"

"Yes, they offered me the job. Head chef."

"That's what you wanted, right?"

"I thought so."

"But?" She lowered her chin but lifted her eyes as she studied his shift of expressions. What inner battle was he fighting?

He cupped her cheek. "It felt kind of empty without you by my side. I love you, Emma. I'm sorry it took me a minute to figure that out."

"A minute?" She smiled with her sarcasm.

He lowered his head and captured her lips in a tender kiss. "Okay, a day."

She did a playful push against his chest. "Sounds about right."

His expression turned serious. "Will you forgive me for being such a dope?"

"Yes, and I'll even let you make it up to me." She kept her tone light, but she meant what she said—she forgave him. But trusting him would take some time.

Manny tugged her closer, leaning in for another kiss. She should tell him she loved him, especially now that he'd professed his love for her.

So why hadn't she? And why did she feel relieved his kisses gave her an excuse for not saying it back?

———————

After checking the details of his information to make sure he'd followed the guidelines to the letter, Calen clicked the submit button. A thank you message popped up, telling him he should hear from their editors within a couple of weeks. And due to the volume of submissions they received, if he heard nothing within that time, that meant they'd passed on his submission.

Whatever. He made a mark on his calendar so he'd remember when he submitted his pieces. Who knew? Maybe he'd wind up with his first publication by the end of the summer.

He left his office and headed back to the front of the shop. Steph stood at the register, helping a customer. Two of the tables needed bussing, so he grabbed a tray and a rag.

As he cleared the second table, the bell on the front door jingled. He glanced over his shoulder and almost dropped the tray of dirty dishes.

Emma stared at him with the most forlorn expression he'd ever seen on her adorable face. He made himself breathe and straightened to face her. "Hey there."

Dressed in a tank top with a cute pair of floral shorts, she lifted one arm to give him a hesitant wave. She held his journals on her hip with her other one. "Hi. Can we talk?"

He'd dreaded this, but the sooner they cleared the air and figured out if it was still breathable, the better. "Sure."

Calen slid the tray of dirty coffee cups onto the back

counter by the sink and waved Emma to follow him. "We can talk in my office."

Steph raised a brow at him.

He ignored her unspoken question. "Be back in a few."

After Emma followed him in, he signaled to the one chair and shut the door.

"I'd rather stand, if that's okay."

"Sure, whatever you need." He could do this, couldn't he? Go back to the friend zone and return to normal? He leaned against the side desk by his printer. The confirmation of his magazine entry sat in the top tray. He flipped it over.

She noticed his actions and gave him a questioning look.

"Just some last-minute stuff for your show." When would it stop being so painful to be this close to her, knowing they'd shared a kiss once and never would again? Could he shut that door to his heart when it clamored to be left wide open?

The silence spanned between them.

Emma held out the journals. "I wanted to bring these by. That's all but two of them. I hope you don't mind if I finish reading those."

"Sure. No problem." He put the stack on his desk, acutely aware that Emma had read some of his deepest thoughts.

Her eyes turned glassy. "They're beautiful, Calen. Your poetry made me cry sometimes."

He felt like the awkward dork he was in high school again. "Thanks."

"And you're not passionless." Her voice broke and released a flood of tears down her cheeks. "I never should have said that. I'm so sorry."

Without thinking, he launched himself off the desk to hug her. "Hey, it's okay. I already forgave you for that. And

I'm sorry for what I said about your father. I shouldn't have crossed that line."

She leaned her head back to look up at him. "But you were right. I thought meeting the right guy would make that pain go away, but what you said helped me see I hadn't dealt with it. Now I have."

"You did?"

"Yeah. I even talked to my mom about it. She clarified some things for me too. Turns out my real father didn't leave because of me, but because of him. He didn't feel like he was enough for his family." Her eyes cleared of any lingering tears.

"Wow, that's so sad."

"I know." The blue of her irises appeared a darker blue than normal. "By the way, Mom says hello."

He nodded. Instinctively, his gaze dropped to her lips as the warmth of her hands on his chest seeped through his shirt and registered in his brain.

She didn't move, but he could see her pulse had elevated at the base of her neck.

He stepped back and cleared his throat. "That's really great, Emma. I'm happy for you."

She ran her hands down the front of her shorts. "Thank you."

"For what?"

"For all that you're doing for the show. Manny really appreciates it too."

"So, you two are back together?" He steeled himself against the ache.

She nodded. "He came by the studio last night. We talked for a long time."

"Is he taking the job in New York?"

"That's part of what we're trying to work out." She gave

him that grin that meant she had a bone to pick with him. "He told me about your conversation, too."

He suppressed a groan with his exhale and waited for her reprimand.

"Thank you for looking out for me." She tucked her chin in an obvious attempt to hide her emotions, but not before a couple of tears fell, dotting her tank top.

"Of course, Emma. It's what I do, right?" He tried to lighten things, for her sake, even though his heart felt like it just self-imploded. They were 'working things out.' Probably code for figuring out if Emma would go to New York with him.

"I better get going. I still have one painting to finish and another one to complete before the show."

He leaned against the desk again and crossed his arms. "Right."

She opened the door, but then stopped and turned toward him again. "Are we okay?"

"Always." He grinned but looked away so she wouldn't see the ache ripping him apart.

Once she left, he closed the door, slumped into his chair, and tilted his head back.

Maybe Emma moving to New York would be the best thing for him, too. Because he didn't know how he would survive another encounter like that one.

Chapter Twenty

With the art show just days away, Emma fought to keep her mind from spiraling into a state of panic. She had one piece left…she could do this. Of course, she could do this.

She picked up her phone to text Calen an SOS and hesitated. Since their talk in his office, she hadn't seen Calen and their texts had become sporadic. Not at all like things used to be, with sometimes hourly accounts of ironic humor, minor disasters, and woeful complaints painted with humor.

She missed that. So much. She missed how things used to be between them and blamed herself again for messing their friendship up. Some things just couldn't be undone. Too bad they didn't have an undo button for life. She vaguely remembered Calen saying the same thing and laughed to herself.

Maybe she should text Manny instead. Or call him. Just hearing his voice had a calming effect on her.

She dialed his number, but the call redirected to his voice mail right away. Instead of leaving a message, she hung up. She checked her watch. He hadn't started his shift yet, so she didn't know why he couldn't talk. Just hoped he'd call her back when he had time.

Painting would help. She put the blank canvas she'd prepared for the last piece on her easel and prepared a palette of colors. Next, she selected three brushes, two of which she slipped into her bun, the other in her hand, ready to start.

But, she'd forgotten water to clean her brushes and didn't bring any bottled water with her. She put everything down and grabbed her cup to make the trek down the hall to the ladies' room. Her brain raced with every step, and her heart kept up the pace. Too late to cancel on the art show and she didn't want to. Somehow, she'd get through this. And it would be worth all the worry and anxiety. That's what she'd keep telling herself.

As she neared the restroom, she recognized Calen's voice on the opposite side of the hall. Her curiosity drew her to Mav's studio.

Calen leaned over a workbench, pointing to a sheet of paper. Mav also had his head bent, studying the sketch with a bent knuckle held to his mouth.

He dropped his hand and grabbed a drafting pencil, which made scratching sounds as he drew lines over the sketch. "Did you think of doing it this way?"

Calen held his chin as he watched Mav. He had his hair pulled back into a small man-bun, and looked amazing. She knew he would. The look suited his facial structure and gave him a bit of a mysterious look. Just like the poet he was.

She couldn't look away, just continued to watch how he moved and interacted with Mav. The way his biceps pulsed when he leaned on the table. His laugh of excitement when Mav finished. "That's even better!"

As he stepped back, he noticed her standing there and locked eyes with her.

"Hey, Emma." His voice deepened as he said her name. Did he always sound like that when he said her name? Since they'd hung out little over the last two weeks and things still felt so awkward, she wasn't sure.

She did a mental shake to her addled brain. First, she forgets water, and now how to talk? "Hey...hope I'm not interrupting."

Mav bounced his gaze between them before settling back on the sketch. "No, just working out some final details on this—"

"A display for my shop." Calen flipped the paper over.

Mav drew his brows together. "Right. A display."

Walking toward her, Calen frowned and tilted his head, but his eyes appeared guarded. "Are you okay?"

She clutched the cup in front of her. "Yeah, sure. Just needed some water for my brushes." She held up the cup.

"How's it going? Almost ready?"

"Almost." She didn't mean for her voice to sound like a startled mouse. Emma took a quick breath and exhaled through pursed lips.

His expression softened as he took the cup from her. "Hey, if you don't mind, can I come watch you paint for a bit? I don't have to be at the shop until this afternoon."

Warmth spread through her chest, loosening that tight feeling in her muscles. Calen to the rescue again. She loved how he knew how to navigate her anxiety in front of others so as not to draw attention to it.

Another thing she loved about him.

Loved...about him...?

There were lots of things she appreciated about her best

friend. Nothing odd about loving him, right? He was a great guy. An amazing friend…

"I'd love that."

He gave her a quick smile. "I'll head your way when I finish up here."

"Great." She paused, composed herself against the rush of gratitude that nearly brought her to tears. "Thank you, Calen."

He paused and looked at her with an expression that let her know he understood what she didn't say. "Of course."

He waited until she left Mav's studio and heard the ladies' room door open, then shut to exhale and rather loudly at that.

"Wow."

Calen had almost forgotten Mav was in the room. He spun around. "What?"

Mav nodded in the direction Emma had gone. "You two are really into it, aren't you?"

Calen shook his head. "Not at all. She's with Manny."

"You sure about that, man? Only one reason a woman looks at a guy like that. Trust me, I know."

"What look? What are you talking about?"

Mav studied him a moment before his expression shifted to one of sudden realization. "Oh, you really don't see it, do you?"

"There's nothing to see." He didn't need Mav trying to open the door he'd carefully locked and lost the key for. Manny was back and loved Emma. That door would not open again, and he needed to leave it be. For his own sanity.

Mav cocked his head, showing his disbelief. "If you say so."

After Calen finished working out the details for the sign for Emma's display—he'd commissioned Mav to duplicate Emma's signature from her paintings so he could hang it near her pieces to identify her—he headed down the hallway to her studio.

Emma sat in front of her easel, staring at a blank canvas with a near terrified expression on her face. She didn't move when he walked in. Nor did she swivel her head when he brought a chair over and sat next to her. And when he took her hand in his, she still stared at the blank canvas.

Reminded him of his early days out of college when he had a writing deadline. Nothing worse than a blank page staring back.

Or a blank canvas, it seemed.

"You can do this, Emma. I believe in you completely."

She squeezed his hand. "You always have, haven't you?"

Her question came across so serious…and almost sad. Probably just her chaotic mind. "Of course. That's what friends do."

She spun her head to face him. Her eyes appeared paler than normal, which usually happened when she was stressed out. "My best friend…"

"Who's a guy." He grinned. Humor usually helped snap her out of it.

She rewarded him with a quick, soft chuckle, but her gaze turned serious. "Correction. Who's a *great* guy."

He didn't know what to say, and even if he did, his heart had leaped so far up his throat that he couldn't speak.

"I knew you'd look great in a man bun. Like the true poet you are." She reached up and touched his hair.

Her touch sent his pulse and his longing for her back

into overdrive. And just about the time he neared losing his resolve to squash down his feelings for her, she picked up her brush and began painting.

As she guided the brush across the canvas, she drifted away into her work. Her breathing leveled out, and she looked peaceful. Painting always brought her to that place —her happy place. Everything about her shifted into a keen focus that poured out in her unique creative expression. The colors she created inspired him with words. Too bad he didn't have his journal with him.

Calen lifted his attention to the clock on her wall. Thirty minutes had passed in what felt like five. He loved watching her while she painted. In her groove.

Who was he kidding? He just loved watching her. But he'd better leave before he wanted more.

He stood as quietly as possible so as not to disturb her. And he almost made it to the door before she called his name.

"Calen?"

He spun around. "Yeah?"

"Thanks again." Her expression held the fullness of her gratitude. No mistaking that.

"No problem." He closed the door behind him, then leaned his head against the doorjamb, never imagining that the friend zone could be so torturous.

Chapter Twenty-One

Satisfied with the progress of the painting, Emma felt more at ease and able to leave her studio for the day. She'd finish this last piece in plenty of time for it to cure.

She sighed as she dropped her keys in the bowl by the door and let her bag drop from her shoulder to the floor. Manny said he would try to stop by after work tonight, but she honestly wasn't sure if she could stay awake that late.

But she would do her best. They needed time together to figure out if they had a future.

Her stomach rumbled, reminding her she hadn't eaten since breakfast and her fridge had little to offer at the moment, except for sandwich fixings.

Once she threw something together, she sat on the couch, but when she reached for the TV remote, Calen's last two journals grabbed her attention. She took a bite of her sandwich and flipped one open.

Calen's words flowed on the page differently in this journal. She glanced up to the date at the top of the page—these entries were his more recent work. A cohesion she'd not noticed in his other work rose with rich clarity in his prose. Yet the common theme of space showed up again.

As she continued to read, she felt drawn into his poetic storytelling of a lone planet looking for its sun. He searched the galaxy for her, encountering moments of her lingering light and warmth which led him in his search to find her.

A knock on her door made her jump. She'd totally lost herself in Calen's words and hadn't even finished her sandwich.

As she opened the door, Manny's familiar cologne and smile greeted her. They stared at each other as if shy and meeting for the first time. "Hi there."

"Hi." He brought his hand from behind his back and held out a red rose. "I know it's kind of cliché, but I want to do this right."

She took the rose from him as he leaned closer. Her heart kicked into high gear.

"I love you, Emma Price." His eyes sparkled with his intensity as he leaned in to kiss her, sweet and tender. He lifted his head. "Can I come in?"

She gave a nervous laugh. Why was she feeling unsettled? "Sure."

After closing the door, she walked to her kitchen to find a vase. This rose marked his first, in person declaration of love. She'd dry it in a book before it wilted and add it to her memory box. "I don't care if it's cliché. I love it."

"I have great news too." He held his hands together with excitement. "They took my wanting to think about the offer as bargaining and sweetened the deal."

She set the vase and rose on the counter. "Oh?"

"Not only do they want me to be head chef, but they also want to give me carte blanche to design the entire restaurant—the menu, the staff, the interior. Everything.

Plus, they're giving me ten percent ownership as a sign-on bonus. Can you believe it?"

They hadn't even talked about whether he would take the job yet, and now the stakes had increased.

"That's great, Manny." She tried to sound excited, but she sounded hesitant, even to herself.

He took her hands and tugged her close. "Come with me, Emma. I want you by my side for this. You can help me design the restaurant." His excitement built. "And we can even use some of your artwork, like the painting you did of me."

Before the wedding, she would have said yes in a heartbeat, but now? Nothing felt sure anymore. The thought of leaving everything she knew to start over in a new place—especially a place like New York—overwhelmed her. Her heart raced and her chest did that tightening thing she hated.

She brushed past Manny to sit down on the couch.

Manny followed her but stood on the other side of the coffee table. "Aren't you going to say anything?"

She pursed her lips to exhale. "Sorry, it's just a lot all at once."

He sat next to her and took her hands. "I'm sorry. I forget sometimes that you can only take a little excitement at once."

Why did his words hold an edge of condescension? Maybe she was imagining it. Or exaggerating it in her head. That happened when she became panicked.

She closed her eyes for a moment and inhaled. No reason to get upset. They could figure this out. "I thought we were going to talk about all this before you made a final decision."

He held his hand out. "That's what we're doing now. And why I came early. So we could talk and make plans."

But hadn't he said the *something important* was to tell her he loved her in person? "I thought this was about you telling me how you feel."

"Yes, that too." His smile slipped a bit. "Can't it be both?"

She did a quick shake of her head and clasped her hand into his. Why was she being silly? "Yes, of course."

His smile went to high beam. "Good. So, will you come with me?"

She swallowed down the dread lodged in her throat. "Can I think about it?"

He pulled his head back. "I thought this was what you wanted?"

"What I wanted most was for you to say you love me, but now…" Her voice trailed off as she tried to collect her thoughts.

"And I do, Emma. I do love you. I said I was sorry for being an idiot and not realizing it sooner."

She clasped his hand. "It's not that. And I forgive you. I just need some time to think about what it all means."

He studied her for a moment, then cupped her cheek. "I'll ask them to give me a little more time, okay?"

She nodded just before he leaned in to kiss her again. He pulled her closer and just held her while they watched a movie together, which reminded her of movie nights with Calen. She tried to lose herself in the movie to relax, but Manny would pause the movie every time something reminded him of his recent trip to New York and set her nerves on edge again.

Emma tried her best to sound engaged and interested,

would be much easier if they would get on board with moving on like he was.

Okay, trying to do.

He drove to the warehouse so he could load the metal signature into his trunk. But first... Emma. He steeled his nerves and shoved his heart into the vault.

Her door stood ajar. As he drew closer, Manny's voice filtered into the hallway. "Why is this such a big deal? I don't understand."

Calen froze, unsure whether to leave or wait around in case Emma needed him.

"I'm trying to explain, Manny. You told me you wanted to talk about this, but in reality, you just wanted to tell me about the decision you already made. Be honest, you already decided to move back to New York."

"Not really, but how can I refuse now that they're offering me a contract with an opportunity to develop a chain of restaurants?"

Emma's voice softened. "You can't. And I wouldn't want you to."

"Then come with me." Manny's voice pleaded.

"Do you really want that?"

"Yes. Don't you?"

The pause lingered.

"I don't know. Things just seem...different now." Emma's reply brought him to a halt. Had her feelings for Manny changed?

"Is this about Calen?"

"What? What are you talking about?"

"Come on, Emma. Can't you see the guy is nuts about you?"

Calen spun around and sprinted back the way he came. No way would he get caught in the hallway after that one. And he didn't think he could handle her answer right now.

Did some part of him still hold hope that Emma would realize she loved him?

He ducked into Mav's open door.

Mav turned off his torch, pushed his helmet shield back, and furrowed his brows at him. "Something going on that I need to know about?"

"Not really."

"Good. I'm almost done with your sign. Just give me a few minutes." He dropped the shield again and restarted his torch.

Calen nodded and turned around, looking at the empty hallway. Did he venture back toward Emma's studio and see if she was okay? What if she believed Manny and asked Calen if it was true? He really didn't want to have that conversation yet.

But his concern for Emma propelled him back toward her studio. He faltered when Manny shot out of Emma's doorway and headed toward him in a fast stride. His gaze locked onto Calen for a few seconds, but he didn't stop. Just strode past Calen with a scowl on his face.

Calen glanced over his shoulder, then quickened his step to Emma's studio.

She stood in front of the counter where she'd lined up her paintings for the show, arms crossed and lost in thought.

He cleared his throat to let her know he was there.

She swiveled her head to look at him. "Hi."

"Hey there." He braved a few steps closer to her. "I saw Manny leave…he looked pretty upset. Are you okay?"

"You ask me that a lot these days." She gave him a wan smile.

"Just concerned."

She let out a sarcastic laugh. "You know me. My relationships always crash and burn at some point. This one just took a little longer."

"I'm sorry." He didn't know what else to say to her right now. In the past, he'd navigated her breakups as the doting best friend, but his heart couldn't function that way. Not yet.

"Don't be. I'll survive. I always do, right? Thanks to you." Her stare lingered; as if she was asking him for something.

But what could he say? She needed to get over Manny and figure things out first.

"All right, then I'll be on my way. Lots to get done before the show." His upbeat tone sounded forced, even to himself.

She dropped her gaze as she sighed. "Thank you again for all of that. Really."

"My pleasure." This time he was the one who stared— at the brushes poking out of her messy bun, at the way the tendrils of hair around her face fell forward as she played with the cord tied in a bow at the top of her shorts, and the soft curve of her tanned shoulders offset by the bright pink of her tank top. "Free for dinner tomorrow evening? My treat."

She seemed to perk up at his invitation. "I'd love that."

"Good. I'll pick you up at six." Wait until she saw who he was bringing with him. He'd hatched this surprise as a last-minute thought, but everything had worked out.

He made it halfway down the hall to Mav's when he remembered he never told Emma his news.

His favorite poetry magazine wanted to publish his work. And not just one piece, but an entire series.

Chapter Twenty-Two

After Calen left, Emma finished up the last painting and left it to dry overnight. In the morning, she'd examine her pieces with fresh eyes and do any last-minute touch-ups before she had to take the pieces to the gallery. But overall she was pleased with her work.

As to the art critics Manny invited, she had no control over how things would play out there. In light of their breakup, she'd like to believe Manny wouldn't do something vicious, like tell them not to come, but people did strange things when they felt rejected. She could pull a few stories out of her own past...

But she doubted he would do something that would jeopardize his own future.

Tired of her jumbled thoughts, she flopped down on the couch and grabbed the TV remote. Mr. Bean was on the menu, as well as the Chinese food she'd picked up on her way home.

But Calen's journal sat there, open to the last place she'd

read. She took a bite of an egg roll and wiped her hands before she flipped the page to the next entry, dated several weeks ago—the night of their double date.

He'd jotted down the lyrics to 'You're My Satellite.' After that Calen shifted to speaking of the work of art, questioning if it was what he thought—love in its purest form. Self-less, self-sacrificing, always protecting…

Always protecting…Calen did that to the point of driving her nuts. He even punched out Manny when he thought—

Wait…

Manny had said Calen was nuts about her. Could he be right?

She picked up the journal and sat back on the couch, continuing to read Calen's interpretation of the song. He spoke of the sun as *the first star he ever found and would ever orbit around*.

Emma dropped the journal and jumped up from the couch. Calen had written her a poem years ago in high school after that horrific dance.

She rushed into her bedroom. Her memory box still sat open on the floor. She rummaged through the contents until she found the folded piece of paper.

One line of the old poem stood out.

You're my sun, Emma Price, a prize of great price.

She laughed. Back then, she'd rolled her eyes at how cheesy his wording had been. He'd definitely improved with age.

And I, Calen Cooper, will forever be your satellite.

She blinked, read the line again, then covered her gaping mouth with her hand. In high school, she'd taken it to mean he would always be her friend, always there for her.

But now…what if…could he…?

And if he did…did she?

She dropped her hand and stared at nothing as she tried to figure herself out.

Even when Manny came back, she'd found herself thinking of Calen. Of their kiss, how she felt in his arms—safe, protected. And how he'd responded. Though hesitant at first, he'd taken control of the kiss. And when it turned more intense, he'd pulled back, not her.

She touched her lips. Instead of feeling awkward, everything about that kiss had felt right. Could she be falling for her best friend?

When Norman had shared about his wife being his best friend, she'd thought of Calen right away. What if, deep down, she'd wanted more?

No wonder things felt different with Manny…

And if Calen had feelings for her, why hadn't he said something to her?

Her heart thumped harder as she tried to sort through all her thoughts. She shifted into awareness of her breathing and closed her eyes. And pictured Calen, like she always did.

But instead of the usual image of her best friend, she pictured the Calen who caught her at the wedding. The Calen who kissed her back when she threw herself at him in her kitchen. The Calen who sat next to her as she painted her last piece, encouraging her without saying a word.

Emma jerked to a sitting position on her bed. That was the Calen she wanted to paint. She hopped off her bed and grabbed her purse and keys to go back to her studio. Her dinner sat mostly untouched on the coffee table. She gathered the containers back into the sack and paused as she stared at Calen's journals.

She grabbed those, too.

Time to show Calen just how much he meant to her, and she knew exactly how she would do it.

———————

The glass doors leading to the concourses of the airport whooshed open with the latest arrivals. Calen caught a glimpse of Emma's parents following a young couple holding hands. Of course, he thought of Emma at the site of the woman's blonde hair gathered into a messy bun on her head. But what captured his attention most was the way she looked at her partner.

He wanted Emma to look at him that way one day. But maybe he should accept that was an empty dream at this point and move on. He wasn't Emma's type—he should know that by now.

Emma's mother wrapped him in a bear hug. "Calen Cooper, I can't believe you have a man bun."

He grinned. "Blame your daughter. It was her idea."

Her father gave him a knowing look. "And you obliged her?"

Calen held his hands out. "You do know your daughter, right?"

On the way down the escalator to the luggage carousels, they chatted about Tuscon, where they'd retired a few years ago.

Mrs. Price linked her arm with Calen's. "I'm so glad you called and asked us to come."

"Of course. I know Emma will be thrilled that you flew in for her show."

"I just don't understand why she didn't tell us what a big deal this is."

"You know Emma. She doesn't give herself enough credit as an artist."

Mrs. Price craned her neck up as she patted his shoulder. "You're such a good friend, Calen. You have no idea."

Mr. Price hefted one of their suitcases off the conveyor belt while pointing to another. "Grab that one, would you?"

Calen jumped forward. "No problem."

Mr. Price kept his voice low. "You sure Emma will be okay with this? I don't want to overwhelm her."

"Are you kidding? She'll be thrilled."

"Even with this breakup?"

Calen appreciated Mr. Price's concern for Emma. "She's doing really well, actually. Surprised even me. But I still think having dinner with her before the show will help keep her from being overwhelmed by too much happening at once."

Emma's father nodded and gave him a reassuring grin.

Calen drove them to their hotel in downtown Sarasota, which would put them within walking distance of the gallery and his shop. He'd printed out a map and circled the locations along with a few others for them to explore in their free time.

"If you need anything, just call. I'm right around the corner. And I'll pick you up tomorrow at five-thirty, then we'll pick Emma up at her place."

Her mother clasped her hands. "She's going to be so surprised."

After saying goodbye, Calen headed to his car. Should he check on Emma and make sure she wasn't in some kind of meltdown? He hadn't heard from her all day and he'd lost track of time with final preparations for the preview show. He wanted to have a backup plan in case Manny bailed out on his part, which he dearly hoped the man did not. Calen didn't want to have to punch the guy out again.

He sent a text to see if Emma was doing okay. The moving dots appeared right away and then her 'At my studio working on a last-minute piece' appeared.

No binging Mr. Bean and no mounds of soggy tissues. What had happened to his best friend?

Chapter Twenty-Three

The morning sunshine that normally gave her the best light for painting blasted her awake. She'd worked on the new piece through most of the night and then crashed on the lounger, too tired to drive home.

She stretched out the kinks of sleeping on the bumpy cushion and made her way to where the painting still sat on her easel. Would she love it as much as she had last night? Painting Calen had brought an astounding rush of emotion that built to a flood of tears as she finished the piece.

As she studied his image, tears welled in her eyes again.

She loved it.

She loved Calen.

With each brush stroke, she'd discovered more feelings she held for him and fell more in love with him.

How had she missed this? Missed him all these years in her search for the right guy?

He'd been there all along.

She had one more task to accomplish before she could

go home and clean up. Emma left her studio and headed down the hall.

Maverick stood by his workbench, studying some kind of magazine.

She knocked on the doorframe.

He turned to face her. "Hey there."

"I was wondering if you could help me with something."

"What might that be?"

"I need something to display a journal. A pedestal of some sort. Or podium. Have you got one lying around that you don't need?" She gave him a hopeful smile.

He crossed his arms and tilted his head. "You look like you slept here."

"That's because I did. Working on a last-minute piece for the art show."

"And now you need a stand for it?"

"No, it's for one of Calen's journals."

"Because..."

She played with the string tie of her shorts. "I want to display his journal in the show. It's part of this last piece I did."

Maverick quirked up one side of his mouth. "Does he know about this?"

"No, and I'd appreciate it if you didn't tell him anything. It's a surprise."

He nodded as he studied her. "Okay, I think I can help with that." He brushed past her, jingling his keys as he crossed the hallway and unlocked a door near the restrooms.

She followed him in. "You lease two spaces?"

He moved several large metal pieces out of the way.

"Not exactly. Just borrowing the space until I can get this project finished and delivered. The owner's a friend."

"Ah, then maybe you can put a good word in for me about a sink. I want one in my studio, so I don't have to constantly send my students to the bathroom."

He laughed out loud. "I can mention it to him."

"Thanks." She tried not to roll her eyes and stayed near the door and out of the way.

Maverick leaned over and dragged out a wrought iron frame that looked like the base of a stool. "How about this? I can clean it up and add a piece on the back part so you can tilt the book up a bit."

"That would be amazing. You don't mind?"

As he lifted the stool onto his shoulder, he shot her a side glance. "No, not at all. Calen's a good guy."

"Yeah…he is." She clasped her hands at her waist and followed him back to his studio. "I really appreciate your help. Let me know what I owe you."

"I'll have it finished this afternoon. No charge." He laid the stool on his workbench.

"No, I want to pay you for your work. Artists need to support one another."

He gestured to the stool. "Is that what this is about?"

"Yes, I want to share Calen's poetry in the show."

He chuckled. "I knew you liked him."

"Excuse me?" She'd barely spoken to Maverick in the last year, let alone the entire two years since he moved in, yet he thinks he knows how she feels about Calen? "What makes you say that?"

"It's pretty obvious."

"Wish it had been to me." She muttered her words as she turned to leave.

"He's nuts about you too, by the way."

She stopped, turned around, and pointed at the stand. "I hope you're right. Otherwise, this is going to flop in the worst way."

"It won't." He started wiping down the metal with a cloth.

"How do you know?" The man had more confidence than a pit bull, which he kind of reminded her of with his swaggering demeanor and lopsided grin.

"What's your gut telling you?"

"I'm hungry?"

He laughed. "Okay, what's your heart telling you?"

"Interesting question coming from a welder."

"Hey, we have feelings too." His voice held a teasing tone.

"Sorry." She let out a noisy breath. "I'm still trying to figure that out."

"That's a good start."

She started to leave but turned around again. "If Calen comes by, don't tell him about any of this, okay?"

"You got it."

"Thanks, Maverick. I'll come by and pick it up this afternoon."

He gave a thumbs-up after he slipped his welding mask onto his head.

Back in her studio, Emma stood in front of the painting of Calen. "You and I are going to have a serious talk tonight."

"We'll stand off to the side so she doesn't see us right away. That'll make the surprise even better." Mrs. Price clapped her hands in pure delight, just like Emma did when she was super excited over a plan she hatched. Mr. Price kept a perpetual grin on his face like a dolphin.

Emma would love this. He hoped...

He knocked, tucking his chin as he waited. The tap of heels sounded closer, then the door opened. There she stood, dressed in a stunning teal dress that made her eyes look bluer, her hair swept up in a not-so-messy bun, minus the paintbrushes, and heels.

She'd dressed up...why had she dressed up? Did she know about her parents? Good thing he'd traded his jeans for a pair of charcoal slacks and a white button-down.

"Wow."

Her smile exploded and completed her ensemble. "Glad you like it."

"You look...amazing." He'd expected her usual casual attire. Not this.

She moved closer, filling his senses with a flowery, musky scent. "Do we need to leave right away, or do we have time to talk first?"

Mr. Price cleared his throat behind them.

Emma leaned her head to the side. "Dad?"

Calen turned and stepped back so she could see her parents.

Mr. Price gave her a sheepish smile. "Hey, peanut."

Mrs. Price waggled her fingers at her. "Surprise."

Emma shot a glance at him, eyes glassy, before she rushed forward to her parents and hugged them. "I can't believe you're here!"

Mr. Price kissed the top of her head. "We wouldn't miss it."

"I'm so glad Calen called and asked us to come. We

didn't know it was such a big deal." Pride in her daughter covered Mrs. Price's face.

Emma leaned back from their huddle. "I guess it is."

Her mother cupped her cheek. "Of course it is."

Calen checked his watch. "We'd better get going if we want to make our reservation."

As Emma and her parents walked toward his car, Emma glanced over her shoulder and mouthed 'thank you' to him while her mother chatted away about how excited they were to see her first official art show.

On the drive to the restaurant, Emma sat in the back with her mother and behind her father in the passenger seat, which allowed him to see her in the rear-view mirror. Every opportunity he had, Calen glanced up to check out her reflection.

Emma took his breath away. He almost regretted his surprise because he wanted nothing more than to have her to himself. And what did she want to talk to him about? Was she having second thoughts about Manny? Did she want to move to New York after all?

His gut and chest tightened at the thought. He glanced at the mirror again. Emma caught him this time. And smiled at him, but not like her usual I'm-glad-to-see-my-best-friend way. Was she…flirting with him?

"Light's green." Mr. Price's voice snapped him back to attention.

"Thanks." He pressed the gas.

Calen parked right on Pineapple Avenue, almost in front of Kaleena's place and just a couple of doors down from Madilyn's Grill & Wine Bar. He lagged behind, giving Emma and her parents space to reconnect. As they walked by Sass & Sun Fashions, Kaleena waved to him from the other side of the front display window, then gave him a thumbs-up.

So far, the evening was a tremendous hit, but he still couldn't shake the feeling that Emma was about to drop a bombshell on him.

Chapter Twenty-Four

Throughout dinner, Emma kept stealing glances at Calen. He looked so good in charcoal gray and white, especially the way he had his sleeves folded up to his forearms. She loved his easy and confident manner, which seemed to increase her attraction to him.

She never imagined seeing Calen like that, but here she was, wishing they were alone so they could talk. So she could tell him she'd figured out she was his muse and in doing so, he'd become hers.

Nope, never could have imagined this happening to them in a million years...

And she still couldn't get over what Calen had done. To call her parents and arrange this surprise? She didn't realize how much she wanted them here for the show until she saw them.

But Calen knew...

As they stood to leave, something in her peripheral vision caught her attention. Manny stood in the back of the restaurant, staring at her.

Calen came over and stood next to her. "I'm sorry, Emma. I thought Manny had left for New York already."

"Me too." Seeing Manny tugged at her heart a bit, but not like she thought it would. "Give me a minute, okay? I'll meet you outside."

Slipping his hands into his pockets, he nodded and flatlined his mouth. "Sure thing."

Emma made her way around tables to where Manny stood.

His slow smile greeted her. "You look so beautiful tonight."

"Thank you." She dropped her gaze for a moment. "How are you?"

He sighed. "Okay, I guess. Getting ready for my move."

"When do you leave?"

"Day after tomorrow. I delayed my flight so I could be at your show."

"You did?"

He nodded. "Plus, I kind of made a commitment to provide the hors d'oeuvres."

A soft laugh bubbled up, which felt good. She didn't want things between them to be awful. Manny was a great guy. Just not the guy for her. "Thank you."

"Of course. I'd do anything for you, Emma." He leaned in and kissed her cheek.

She waited for that rush of attraction to hit her like it usually did when he got that close to her, but she didn't feel any of it. Just the bittersweetness of a goodbye.

"Take care."

"You too." As she walked toward the front of the restaurant, Calen watched her through the front window. Had he seen her entire exchange with Manny? She'd have to explain to him when they talked later.

The sun hadn't started to set yet, but the light had changed and softened in the sun's descent toward evening. The balmy night air settled around them as they walked back to the car. Her parents held hands as they walked ahead of her.

Calen remained silent as he walked next to her.

Her heart raced with the anticipation of telling him what she'd discovered over the last two days—about him and about herself.

At the hotel, Emma hugged her parents good night with the promise of seeing them tomorrow, then got back in the car. Calen remained silent on the trip to her apartment, too.

He parked in front of her place but didn't move to get out of the vehicle.

"Aren't you going to come in? I thought we were going to talk." She'd unbuckled her seat belt and opened her door.

His expression appeared almost sad. "Big day tomorrow. You need your rest and so do I."

She put her hand on his arm. "Please, Calen. This is important."

He sighed. "Okay."

Nervous energy made her steps feel short and quick. She'd imagined multiple ways of this evening playing out and rehearsed in her mind what she wanted to say, but now that the moment had arrived, clarity seemed to flee with her nervousness.

What if she had it all wrong and Calen had actually been writing about Nina?

What if he was right and what she was feeling for him was just a rebound?

What if their friendship wound up tanked with another failed relationship on her part?

Once inside her apartment, she kicked off her heels and dropped her small clutch on the kitchen table.

Calen lingered by the door.

"Do you want a glass of water or something?" She clasped her hands in front of her.

"No, I'm good. Thanks."

"Do you want to sit down?"

He rubbed the back of his neck. "What did you want to talk about, Emma?"

"I wanted to thank you for what you did with my parents."

"You already thanked me."

She shrugged and took a couple of steps toward him. "I know, but I didn't get to tell you how much that meant to me. That you would do that for me."

"That's what best friends do."

Bold courage surged up in her. "Is it?"

"Yes, why?"

"Because it seems like more to me."

He hadn't really looked at her until now. "Like what?"

She closed the gap between them. "That you care about me."

"Of course I do, Emma. I thought that was obvious."

Her throat closed with the upsurge of emotion flooding her heart. She swallowed it down. "It is, but I'm talking about love."

She must have figured out his journals were about her. How could she not? And now she was going to let him down easy.

He'd watched her with Manny at the restaurant;

witnessed the entire exchange. Manny still had it bad for her. That much Calen could see. So he'd prepared himself to hear she'd made the decision to move to New York.

But that did nothing to ease the crushing ache in his chest. He unclenched his jaw so he could speak. "I get it. And I'm not blind. Just say it, Emma."

She frowned at him. "What are you talking about?"

He did a quick shake of his head to show his disbelief that she would throw this back on him. Did he have to say it for her? "That you love Manny and you're going with him to New York."

"What makes you think that?"

"I saw you two at the restaurant. He's still in love with you." Part of him wanted to bolt. The other resigned himself to hearing the truth—she loved Manny and was willing to uproot her life to be with him.

Maybe he would be the one binging Mr. Bean on his couch tonight.

"I guess, maybe. But I'm not in love with him, so I think moving to New York would be a bad idea."

His neck muscles tensed as he locked gazes with her. "Then what are you saying?"

She took a deep breath, then exhaled as she tilted her head. "I read your journals. All of them. And I had an epiphany."

He couldn't help but quirk a grin. "Nice word."

"I know, right?" She moved close enough that he could feel her body heat.

Her eyes made him a prisoner, just like his heart. He wanted to twine the tendrils surrounding her face around his finger and feel the silky softness of her hair. And if she got any closer, he'd kiss her in such a way to make sure she knew their days of 'just friends' were over.

"So what was this epiphany?"

"I'm your muse."

Not what he wanted to hear, but it did make him laugh. "Okay, I confess. It's true."

"I know." Her expression turned serious. "Guess what else I discovered?"

"What?" He breathed his answer.

"You're mine, too." She slid her hands up his arms to the back of his head as she tilted her face up.

Calen didn't hesitate to capture her lips with his. Everything he'd held back over the last several weeks—every desire, longing, ache—burst out and ran free. He wrapped his arms around her and pressed her against him, memorizing the way her body molded to his.

She smelled like the jasmine that bloomed at night mixed with vanilla and musk. While his heart was fully engaged—and his body in all honesty—his mind stuttered on the reality that he held Emma this close and not only was he kissing her, she was kissing him back. Passionately too, as if he was the one she wanted to be with. At least at the moment...

He wanted more. A lifetime of more.

But did she?

He leaned away to break the kiss so they could talk, but she took charge and deepened the kiss again. Next thing he knew, he was on the couch with Emma on his lap. And as much as he was enjoying this, they needed to discuss what this was really about.

He broke the kiss and lifted her to sit next to him.

"Calen, what's wrong?"

He leaned forward and held his head in his hands, willing his heart to slow down. Everything needed to slow down for a minute. He twisted his head to look at her. "Are you sure it's me you want?"

She looked at him like he was crazy. "Is that not obvious?"

He dropped his hands and shifted on the couch to face her. "You just broke up with Manny and now, because you read my goofy poems, you think you have feelings for me?"

"They're not goofy. Your poetry is beautiful." She held his face between her hands. "Calen, you made me cry. I was so blown away. And then when I realized you were writing about me, it was like a light finally went on in my head. And my heart. You've always been there for me, Calen. I love that."

He rose from the couch and stood in the middle of her living room, wanting nothing more than to accept her words as a facsimile of what he wanted to hear—that she loved him. But just like he told Nina he didn't want to be Emma's 'pause for thought,' he also didn't want to be the one she settled for.

Which meant he had to take the risk and be honest about his feelings and what he wanted. "Remember when you asked me what I'm passionate about?"

She jumped up and rounded the coffee table to stand near him. "I shouldn't have said—"

He held his hand up to stop her. "It's you, Emma. It's always been you."

Tears welled in her eyes as she tilted her head and lifted her shoulders in a way that made her look oh so vulnerable and kissable. "I know. Your words said it all."

Seeing her so emotional did weird things to him. He wanted to comfort her, make sure she was okay, but part of him felt the need to protect his heart.

He cupped her face between his hands, scrambling for

words to express his feelings, his fears, and his hopes. "I love you, Emma, but I can't just be your best friend anymore, and I can't just be your next boyfriend."

She wrapped her arms around his waist, her eyes darting back and forth as she searched his face. Her chin quivered as tears dropped from her crystal blue eyes. "Then can you be my best friend—who's a guy—who's also the love of my life?"

His brain and heart stuttered together in a double take. "Great words."

His fear spiraled to the ground and released the protective restraints he'd belted around his heart. He couldn't think beyond his need to hold her close and kiss her with all the love he'd held for her for so long.

At first passionate, the kiss shifted to a tenderness he realized was Emma expressing her love for him and asking for an answer. He lifted his head just enough to speak. "I can be that. I mean, I want to be that. More than you know."

She kissed him before leaning back to look into his eyes again. "There's so much I want to tell you."

They sat back down on the couch, talking and kissing until he noticed how late it was. "I should go so you so can get some sleep."

She yawned. "I know, but I don't want to let you go yet."

"Don't ever let me go." He couldn't resist teasing her.

"Never."

"I have an idea." He grabbed one of the throw pillows behind him and laid back on the arm of the couch, then opened his arms for her to lie down next to him.

She snuggled in next to him and laid her head on his chest. "I don't think I'll be able to stay awake."

"Go to sleep, Emma. I've got you."

In less than a minute, her breathing slowed and her body relaxed. He kissed the top of her head as his own tiredness beckoned to take over.

He fought it long enough to fully comprehend and relish the turn of events of this day. Prose formed in his mind to describe it all as he drifted into sleep.

Chapter Twenty-Five

She woke before dawn, still snuggled against him. Sometime during the night, Calen had tugged his man-bun free and his hair covered part of his face.

Stubble covered his angled jawline and surrounded his full lips. She wanted to kiss him but didn't want to wake him more. As she studied him, she reflected on the painting she'd done of him and realized she'd left something out. Not to do with the essence of how she had painted him, but of his words—his poetry.

An idea sparked.

Emma extracted herself from his hold, trying not to wake him. As she sat up and scooted toward the other end of the couch, he turned on his side and curled his legs up. She pulled the throw from the back of the couch over him.

She changed her clothes, brushed her teeth, and ran a brush through her hair before grabbing her purse and keys. Then thought to leave Calen a note that she'd gone to her studio to do one more thing before the show.

Once there, she opened Calen's journal to the place

where he'd written about her using their song, and composed a reply in her own words.

She added them to her painting in a way to become part of the background yet integrating with Calen's form. Probably not as elegant as his prose, but they were her words that said everything he meant to her.

At least as a start. She had a lifetime to convince him how much she loved him. She sat back from the canvas at the thought…a lifetime.

She and Calen already shared so much life. Years of it. No one knew her better. And for the first time, she wasn't afraid.

Or anxious.

With the last stroke of her brush, she sat back and studied her work. Now the painting felt done. Truly finished.

Once completely dry, she would take it to the gallery to hang with the rest of the pieces she'd taken over yesterday afternoon, along with Calen's journal and the pedestal Maverick had made for her.

In the meantime, she needed coffee and something to eat. She grabbed her wallet, locked up her studio, and walked over to Java Jerry's.

Calen stood behind the counter, working on an order. He wore one of the T-shirts he'd designed for the art preview, as did Steph and the others on duty for the big day. Took everything in her not to let her excitement bubble over and blab what she'd done.

After handing a drink order to his customer, he left the counter and waved her to his office. Once inside, he shut the door and then kissed her. "I have to say I was disappointed I didn't get to do that when I woke up."

"Probably for the best. Morning breath is gross."

He chuckled against her lips. "I think I can handle that."

"Yeah, we'll see about that. Good thing you kissed me before coffee. That's worse."

He didn't say anything, just stared at her.

Why did he look so serious? "What's that look about?"

"When I woke up this morning and you weren't there, for a minute I thought I might have dreamed last night."

She grinned. "Don't worry. You didn't."

"And you're doing okay with all of this?"

She understood what he was really asking. "I'm fine. Better than fine. Not anxious at all."

"And not overwhelmed?"

"Calen, you've never overwhelmed me. Quite the opposite. You're the sun to my galaxy." She giggled.

He chuckled and gave his head a quick shake. "I thought I was your satellite."

"I've upgraded you." She gave him a playful kiss. "And now this star needs some fuel."

"Look at you, using your words."

"I learned from the best."

———

Calen had his team in place, and everything set up on the back patio area of the gallery. He kept looking for Emma with a mix of excitement and concern for her. After her surprise visit at the shop that morning, he hadn't seen or heard from her. And missed her more than he thought possible.

Emma's parents showed up early. Then more people started showing up. He caught a brief glimpse of Manny as he sent out the trays of his special hors d'oeuvres with Calen's staff, but then he retreated to the restaurant.

But still no Emma.

Was she okay? Had the excitement of everything sent her into a panic attack?

He pulled Steph aside. "Keep a watch on things. I need to make sure Emma's okay."

"No problem."

Calen went inside the gallery and made his way to the front. He'd yet to see Emma's work on display because the turnout had kept him and his team hopping already.

Emma stood near the front with her parents. And she looked amazing in a floral wrap dress and sandals. And she had two small paintbrushes stuck in her messy bun.

He came beside her and leaned over to whisper in her ear. "You still have paintbrushes in your bun."

She spun around and hugged him. "I know. I thought it might add a unique touch."

He chuckled. "Clever girl. Have the art critics shown up yet?"

"Don't know. Don't care. I have something more important to do at the moment."

He frowned. "What's more important?"

She took his hand and led him around to the other side of one of the display walls. The first painting he saw was of Manny.

Calen knew it belonged in the show, but seeing it brought back some doubt about where he and Emma stood.

She stopped him, then pointed to a painting on the other side of the display.

A painting of him.

He held her hand as he moved closer. Then he realized what he thought was abstract texture was words.

His words, but not quite. She'd made them her own so that they spoke back to him, declaring him the sun, the moon, and the stars. And she was his satellite.

She was his.

"Emma…"

"And look there." She pointed to a stand with a book on it.

He moved closer for a better look.

Correction. His journal. On a stand. Like she'd done for the high school art show.

He pulled her closer. "I can't believe you did that."

"Why?"

"Because it's your show."

"But you're my muse, so you're part of my show. So that makes it *our* show."

He couldn't believe she would do that for him. "I love you, Emma Price."

She beamed a smile of a thousand suns. "I love you more, Calen Cooper."

He remembered that he'd not shared his news with her yet. "There's something I've been meaning to tell you."

"What's that?"

"My poetry is going to be published."

Her eyes widened to match the circle she made with her mouth, then she bounced up and down, clapping her hands. "Calen! That's amazing! When?"

"Starting next month."

"Starting?"

"A series. They want to do a series."

She kissed him.

Someone cleared their throat.

Calen opened his eyes as he lifted his head.

Mr. Price stood behind Emma. "I wondered when you two would finally figure things out."

Eyes looking somewhat glassy, Emma's mother nodded her head in agreement.

Emma put her arm around his waist as she turned to face them. "I'm the one who had to figure things out. Not Calen." She tilted her head up to look at him. "He knew all along."

He'd always wanted her to look at him that way; like he was the love of her life. And he couldn't imagine not getting rocked by it, even years down the road. He felt like that satellite that was sent on a mission and was now ready and able to fulfill its purpose.

With Emma. Always Emma.

Epilogue

Six months later...

Emma put the canvas she'd prepared on the easel. The gallery showing turned out to be a major success, not only for her but for several of the artists who took part in the show. And now several of her pieces were on display in galleries in New York and Los Angeles.

Calen sat on the lounger, writing in his journal. Probably working on the next piece for his series. The magazine loved his work so much that they wanted to help him publish a book of his poetry. Negotiations were underway.

Emma loved their days together like this. They'd settled into a groove that filled her with so much peace and love. And she hadn't had an anxiety attack in months. That, in and of itself, felt like a miracle.

A miraculous blessing was birthed from two best friends who realized they were also the love of each other's life. Emma shuddered to think about how things might have gone if she'd moved to New York with Manny.

In a way, Calen had saved her from making a huge mistake. Because then she would have missed out on true love. The forever kind of love that kept her safe and in orbit.

She worked the colors on her palette to capture the shade of midnight blue she wanted for this painting—an abstract exploration of space from the eyes of love.

Calen shifted on the lounger, then stood and walked over to stand behind her.

"Wow, that's coming out great."

She lifted her brush from the canvas. "I'm glad you approve. It's an homage to us."

He chuckled. "Nice word."

"I thought so."

"I have some nice words too, you know." His tone turned playful and kind of sexy.

She put her brush down and turned her stool to face him. "And what might those words be?" She never grew tired of him telling her how much he loved her. How long he loved her. And how happy she made him.

Because she felt the same. More than she ever imagined she could.

He held his hand in a fist in front of her. "I'm holding our future in my hand."

As he opened his fist, she gasped. A diamond ring sat in the middle of his palm.

He picked up the ring with his other hand and went down on one knee, holding the ring up. "Emma Price, will you be my satellite forever?"

"Yes!" She controlled herself until he slipped the ring onto her finger and stood up. Then she threw herself into his arms, loving the way they wrapped around her and pulled her against him.

After a lingering kiss, she leaned her head back to look at her best friend and soon-to-be husband. She'd dreamed of this moment countless times over the last few months, yet he'd managed to surprise her.

"Calen Cooper, you are the Prussian blue to my canvas."

He grinned. "*Very* nice words."

She tugged his head down for another kiss. "I knew you'd approve."

Next in the Seashells and Sunsets series

vinci-books.com/holidayarrangement

Christmas lights aren't the only sparks flying this holiday season.

When their friendship is rekindled at a Christmas party, Corinne and Jeremy create a fake relationship to avoid the matchmaking schemes of friends and family. But the true test comes when their exes show up, looking for some Christmas cheer of their own. Will their holiday arrangement be exposed or turn into the best Christmas gift ever?

Turn the page for a free preview…

The Holiday Arrangement:
Chapter One

Despite the pleasant drop in temperature and humidity, the late November air held the familiar scent of Siesta Key Beach, just a few miles away from downtown Sarasota. Jeremy Payne made a mental note to walk the shore Saturday morning.

Noticing his friend cleaning up the remnants of his lunch, he finished the last bite of his burger. "Time to walk."

They gathered sacks and drink cups from the bench at the far side of a courtyard between several shops and a couple of small restaurants.

"Hey, we're throwing a Christmas party, so put it on your calendar." Stephen waited for him to reply with his goofball expression that always reminded him of the actor Kevin James.

Jeremy tossed the remnants of his lunch into the receptacle. A quick burger and fries with his best friend defined his social life these days. His friend knew it. So did his wife.

"Who's asking? You or Allison?"

Stephen took a sip from his soda before tossing it into the garbage as well. "Me, of course." He shrugged. "And Allison."

"I knew it. Thanks, but no thanks. Not interested in another setup."

Stephen held his hands up in mock innocence. "I swear that's not what this is. Allison has always dreamed of hosting a big Christmas party and now that we're settled in our new house, she's swung into full gear."

"But Thanksgiving is next week." They stopped in front of a shop whose front window display boasted Christmas ornaments, miniature trees, and gift boxes with bright red and green bows.

"Christmas has already arrived, in case you didn't notice." Stephen tapped on the window to make his point, then waved apologetically to the clerk whose attention he'd caught. "She's planning it for early December so that more people will be free to come. Before all the office and family parties hit."

"That's a couple of weeks away." Jeremy pushed the crosswalk button.

"That's why I'm asking you now. Allison wants a bunch of people there. And as her husband, I'm obliged to help make her dream come true."

Jeremy laughed. "So that's what I am now? Just a warm body to help fulfill your wife's dream?" The crossing light turned green.

"Come on. Please? I was serious when I said this wasn't a setup. Just a bunch of friends getting together to celebrate Christmas. Besides, Allison learned her lesson after the last debacle that resulted from her attempts at playing matchmaker."

He dearly hoped so. Probably the most awkward

moment of his life to date. He'd never forget the smell of burning polyester for as long as he lived. "About time."

"And she's truly sorry. She had no idea the woman was on the nutty side."

Jeremy stopped and gave Stephen his 'you've-got-to-be-kidding-me' stare. "Did she even know the woman?"

Stephen hunched his shoulders as he lifted his hands. "Kind of."

Jeremy waved him off. "No dice. Count me out."

They'd walked the full length of Main Street in downtown Sarasota and turned around. Their normal routine to justify eating a greasy burger and fries.

"Tell Allison I appreciate the invite. Tell her I have plans or something."

"Do you?"

He hesitated, searching his mental calendar for any commitments. Since his breakup with Sheridan, his social calendar had tanked big time. Guess their years together didn't garner him much loyalty in their social circle. Didn't help much that she'd controlled that aspect of their image in an attempt to become a power couple in the local society. Another reason why they were better off going their separate ways.

"Just come and hang out with your best friend then." Stephen rested his hands on his chest, brows raised and a goofy grin on his face.

He quickened his speed at the next crosswalk to beat the flashing hand, warning him the light was about to change. Maybe that's what he needed, a *life* change. "Who's going to be there?"

"Just friends. I swear. A few neighbors. Allison's best friend, Corinne—"

Jeremy shot him a suspicious look. It was bad enough

that his mother kept trying to set him up with the recently divorced women in her church. He didn't need any more surprise setups or one of those just-happened-to-stop-by sideswipes.

Stephen held his hand out. "Trust me. Allison would never set you up with her best friend."

Jeremy stopped in front of his building and turned to his friend. "So I'm good enough for psycho woman but not her best friend?" Why did he even care?

Stephen frowned at him. "No, that's not it at all. It crosses some agreement they made a few years ago." He paused. "What, are you secretly wanting to be set up?"

"No." Jeremy shook his head and headed to the entrance of his building. Stephen's building was another twenty feet down the walk. He was better off alone, at least for a while. He needed time to figure out what he really wanted out of life. Sheridan had called the shots for so long that he didn't realize how far off course his ship had sailed until too late.

Stephen's voice followed him inside. "Just think about it. You can stop in, have a couple hors d'oeuvre, and leave."

Corinne Carter waited for her mother to sit down at the table before taking the seat opposite her. The restaurant buzzed with the noon crowd. "What did you think I meant?"

Her mother scooted closer to the table. "I don't know. I thought maybe you had a date."

Corinne laughed. "Mom, don't start. I just got settled into my condo and have yet to even meet my neighbors. Let your daughter breathe a little first, okay? Dating is the last thing on my mind right now."

She shook out the cloth napkin and draped it over her lap as the server filled their glasses with ice water. A long drink pushed away the heat of the day. She'd forgotten how warm Florida could still be in late November. Another thing she'd have to readjust to.

"All right. Fine. I'm just trying to help. You've been alone for a while now—"

"Like I said before, being alone doesn't—"

"Doesn't mean you're lonely. Yes, yes, I remember. I just want to see you happy."

She reached out and took her mother's hand, waiting for her to look up from her study of the menu and meet Corinne's gaze. "Mom, I am happy. I'm back in Sarasota, near the best beaches in the world. And my mother."

Her mother gave her a sly grin. "And in that order, I presume."

Corinne dropped her chin in mock despair. "Oy vey."

Her mother covered her mouth as she giggled before turning serious. "I'm so sorry things didn't work out with you and Peter."

Corinne studied her menu as an excuse to keep her eyes diverted. The last thing she wanted her mother to see were the tears she'd yet to shed over her divorce. Their marriage had ended long before the papers had been signed—and they were separated for a good year before that—but the sting of failure still lingered. "It's for the best, Mom. Peter and I both agreed we did our best. Now we both get a fresh start. I even took back my maiden name."

"Good." Her mother smiled and diverted her attention to her own menu.

She still hadn't told her mother about Peter's alcoholism. The years of living in denial. The repetitive roller coaster of rehab and relapse had left her with enough shame to choke a herd of horses. Plus, she'd grown tired of the pity-filled looks from friends and conversations that inevitably circled the circumstantial drain of their failed marriage.

She gulped down half of her water. Moving back to Sarasota really was her chance to start over. Alone. For the first time in her life, she could give her full attention to her marketing career. And in no way did she miss California traffic.

The server returned to their table and took their orders, leaving them to munch on the bread and butter. Corinne tore off one small piece, allowing herself to have a small dose of carbs.

"Have you made plans for Christmas?" Her mother dipped her knife into the butter pat on the table and spread a generous portion on the chunk of bread in her hand. Somehow her mother managed to eat large amounts of bread yet remain thin as a rail. A trait she didn't inherit.

"Just to be with you."

"No company parties?"

"Not that I know of yet. I'll know more once I start on Monday."

"That could be a great way to meet someone."

"Mom, please."

Her mother shrugged. "I'm just saying…"

"I'm not interested in meeting anyone right now."

The server set plates of food in front of them. Corinne dipped a spoon into the bowl of lobster bisque nestled against a salad.

"Are you sure, sweetie?"

"About what?" Creamy goodness exploded over her tongue.

"Meeting someone." Her mother's expression turned evasive, which usually happened when she'd done something without permission. Margaret Carter had a notorious reputation for trying to fix things, especially other people's lives. Corinne had learned to circumvent her mother's tampering as a teenager, so when she and Peter moved to California, she'd breathed a guilty sigh of relief for many years.

Corinne put down her spoon. "Mom, what did you do? Did you set me up?"

"No, of course not." Her mother studied her food. "That's up to the matchmaker."

"The what?!" Her shout brought the full attention of the table of four to their right. She gave them an apologetic smile. "Sorry." Corinne leaned forward, careful to keep her voice to a rough whisper. "Did you say *matchmaker*?"

Her mother gave her a demure nod.

"Mother, why would you do that?! We're not technically Jewish."

Her mother held her hands out. "She's not Jewish. She's Indian, but she said she can work with us."

The Holiday Arrangement:
Chapter Two

The splashes of red that Corinne had noticed when she drove up to Allison's place turned out to be small poinsettias in green pots lining the walkway. Twinkle lights, pine cones, and sparkling red ribbon embellished a garland trimming the double doors, which boasted two oversized Christmas wreaths adorned in a similar fashion.

She had to hand it to Allison. The woman knew how to decorate for the holidays. She pushed the bell, which played a short snippet of Jingle Bells. Corinne resisted rolling her eyes as Allison opened the door.

Allison squealed as she wrapped Corinne in a hug. "You're here! My best friend is back."

Corinne laughed. "I've been back for over a month."

"I know, but it's still sinking in." Allison tugged her into the house.

She gasped at her first glimpse of Allison's home. Christmas baubles and snow globes covered every surface. A nine-foot tree filled one corner of the living area, decorated with a chartreuse green ribbon boasting bright red polka dots. Matching green and red glitter balls dotted the tree along with a plethora of glass icicles. White twinkle lights strobed softly to complete the effect. Just add a soft lens and voilà!

"Wow... Allison, this is amazing." She felt like a kid who stepped into a real-life North Pole setting in a snow globe. "How long have you been working on this?"

"Days. And some nights. But it'll be worth it. Everyone is going to have a fabulous time. I even hired performers."

"You what?" She followed Allison to the formal dining room table. Cakes, cookies, and Christmas candies covered the table in a cluttered mass of sweet delights. She grabbed a red foil-wrapped chocolate kiss and popped it into her mouth.

Allison swatted her hand with a light tap. "Hey now! The party hasn't started yet."

Corinne pointed to her mouth and mumbled over the chocolaty goodness covering her tongue. "It has in here." She swallowed and laughed with her friend. "So why did you want me to come so early, anyway?"

"Because we need to get dressed." Allison grabbed her wrist and started dragging her toward the master suite.

"Wait. What? I am dressed." She glanced down at her red paisley tie-at-the-waist shirt, black capris, and cork wedge heels with black straps. "I already look Christmasy, Allison."

Her friend stopped and batted mock innocent eyes at her. "Didn't I tell you? It's a Christmas costume party."

After tweaking his Santa hat, Jeremy rang the doorbell. He groaned inwardly as Jingle Bells played, announcing his presence. When Stephen had told him to wear a costume, Jeremy had just laughed at him. Another good reason not to go, but then Stephen played the best friend card again after calling him a Scrooge. That just pushed Jeremy to prove him wrong.

He glanced down at his jeans and green Hawaiian shirt with the words "Mele Kalikimaka" intermingled with white Christmas trees, palm trees, and hula girls. That's as much costume as he could muster.

And red socks.

Besides, Jeremy never could turn down a friend in need, and Stephen seemed to really want him present, although he wouldn't say why. He'd never seen Stephen act so "needy," come to think of it. Maybe the party would loosen his friend's tongue.

A cute elf with curled shoes that sprouted bells at the end swung open the door. "Welcome to the party!" She bobbed her head, which made the bell on the end of her stiff pointy hat jingle as well. Her costume reminded him of the grumpy girl elf in the movie *A Christmas Story*. "You're just in time…" she eyed his shirt, "Hawaiian Santa?"

Jeremy gave her a slow grin. "Very good." He tilted his head and pointed at her. "A Christmas Story?"

She giggled. "You're the first one to get it. My dad loves that movie so I thought, why not?"

That movie defined his childhood. Now he felt old. Wait… her father? He felt his grin slip a bit. When did Stephen's oldest daughter grow up? "Katie?"

She giggled again. "Yeah, I didn't think you recognized me."

"I didn't. Now I do. Last time I saw you, you had—"

"Braces and pigtails. I start college in the fall."

"Wow, that happened fast."

"Dad's in the backyard by the grill." She stepped back and swung her hand to invite him in.

"Thanks." He smiled and slipped by her, relieved he'd recognized Katie and avoided a very embarrassing scenario. Not that he had any interest and dating someone younger than him—Sheridan's ten-year difference had felt more like twenty sometimes. And these days, he had a hard time judging women's ages.

He headed to the lanai area. The sooner he got his friend talking and had an hors d'oeuvre, the sooner he could leave.

As he stepped into the house, two costumed guests came rushing down the hall right in his direction. He recognized Allison right away. Then took note of the woman she dragged behind her, dressed as Mrs. Claus.

He'd ream Stephen good when he had a chance for the set-up his wife was about to push on him.

———

Allison fluffed the white fur trim of Corinne's costume. "I knew you'd look good in this."

Corinne frowned at her reflection. "I look like an over-stuffed strawberry Pop-Tart with icing. Seriously, Allison, Mrs. Claus? Way to make a girl feel old."

"Old?" Allison actually looked offended. "I think you look sexy."

She rolled her eyes. "That's just gross. You know that, right?" She started to undo the belt.

Allison stopped her. "No, no, no, please wear it?"

"Why? What I had on was festive enough."

"For me?" Allison sported her famous pouty face, which always succeeded in getting what she wanted—in high school and college. They hadn't called her the blonde bombshell for nothing.

But something seemed off with her best friend. "Allie, what's going on?" She tugged her to the bench in front of the massive king-sized platform bed.

Allison wiggled around in the pink tight dress of her Cindy Lou Who costume. Corinne couldn't wait to see Stephen dressed as her counterpart, the Grinch.

"Is something going on between you and Stephen?"

One of Allison's red pigtail bows fell out. Tears filled her eyes. "Since we moved into the house, Stephen works all the time. He's hardly home for dinner either." Her face bunched into a tortured mass of tears and sobs. "And he just hired a new secretary who's like right out of college. And blonde!"

Corinne hugged her. "I'm sure Stephen's just busy at work right now."

Allie popped off the bench to grab tissues, which she promptly filled with more tears and blubbering. "I don't know... you think so?"

She stood and turned Allie around to face the full-length mirror. Her costume highlighted her curves to perfection. "Hey, have you looked at you? Allie, you're amazing."

Allison shot her a sarcastic expression and pointed to her raccoon eyes.

The doorbell rang as she grabbed a makeup cloth. "Your guests are arriving so let's get you cleaned up and get this party started."

By the time she got Allie cleaned up, there was no time to change back into her own clothes. She'd have to just suck it up and be the Claus. Missus, that is. She buckled the black belt as Allie tugged on her matching slippers and stood.

"Do I look okay?"

The woman could wear potato sacks and look like Coco Chanel. "Stunning. Ready?"

"Oh, wait." Allie grabbed a lipstick from her vanity and grabbed Corinne's chin.

Before Corinne could push her away, Allie had coated her lips with candy apple red lipstick. She frowned at her reflection. Applied to perfection—how did the woman do that?—and as red as her costume.

"There. That's perfect." Allie grinned from ear to ear and batted her inch-long fake lashes. "You look amazing."

"But it's so… red."

"I know. Matches your costume." She grabbed Corinne's hand and tugged her out of the bedroom into the main part of the house. People had started to arrive and mingle around the food table and outside on the lanai.

"Hurry." Allison did as much of a dash as she could in her tight dress.

Corrine's black boots tapped on the tile. As they hit the foyer and living room, a guy in a Hawaiian shirt and a Santa hat walked in. Another quick study and she recognized the pattern—hula girls and palm trees. Typical Florida costume. She tried not to roll her eyes.

Allison stopped in front of him. "Hey, Jeremy! You made it. Have you seen Stephen?"

"No, but Katie said he's by the grill."

"Great." She glanced at Corinne. "I don't think you've met my best friend, Corinne. She just moved back to Sarasota a month ago."

Something about him looked super familiar. He had just a light dusting of gray at his temples and looked like he exercised regularly. And then her mind unlocked a memory all the way back to high school.

Long hair, T-shirts… "Jeremy Payne?"

He did a double-take. "Cori?"

The Holiday Arrangement:
Chapter Three

A flood of memories rushed in all at once. Waiting by the lockers for Cori to put her books away so they could walk together to the cafeteria. Hanging out at Friday night games. Going to the movies with friends. And then the graduation party they ditched to walk the beach.

He shook himself back to reality. "I didn't know you moved back?"

She smiled as she nodded. "Yeah, just a month ago."

Allison glanced between them. "You guys know each other?"

Cori cleared her throat. "Yeah, we were best friends in high school."

"Him?" Allison pointed her thumb at him with an expression of disbelief.

"Hey now." Jeremy frowned at her.

Allison giggled behind her hand. Just like he'd seen Katie do. "I'm just kidding." She bounced her gaze between them. "I need to find Stephen, so I'm enlisting you two as the welcoming committee."

Jeremy started to protest, but Cori smiled and said sure.

An awkward silence hovered between them as Allison dashed off.

Cori busied herself adjusting the buckle of her costume.

Jeremy tucked his hands into his jeans pockets. "So Cori, did I hear you moved to California—with your husband, right?" Could he sound more obvious?

Her head shot up. "Yes, Peter. But we're not together anymore."

"Oh, I'm sorry."

"Don't be. We agreed we did our best, but it just wasn't working. Hadn't for a long time."

She stood there, staring at him as if she expected him to say something.

Why did he feel so awkward around her, like he was back in high school again. He'd grown comfortable with himself and didn't have to work hard to find a date, if he even wanted one. Though after Sheridan, he was in no hurry to jump back into anything. Maybe he just needed a friend more than anything.

"That's good, right? Sometimes it's best to go separate ways."

She tilted her head. "Sounds like you're speaking from experience."

"Yes, last year. It was either get engaged or get a new life. We just wanted different things."

"Together long?"

"Kind of."

"You may as well have been married then." She laughed and then covered her mouth. "I'm sorry. That wasn't very thoughtful."

Jeremy laughed. Some things didn't change. Cori always

did speak her mind and then consider her words later. "It's okay. Long story."

She gave him a smile filled with the warmth and compassion he remembered the first time he asked her out. "It's really great to see you again, Jeremy."

Before he could respond, the doorbell rang. Cori jumped to answer, becoming a cordial Christmas hostess.

And he couldn't tear his gaze away to even see who was at the door. His words 'great to see you too' fell into the abyss of the past. And probably for the best, because he enjoyed seeing her just a little more than he should.

Corinne found Allison sitting at one of the decorated tables out on the lanai. A cold front had moved through during the previous night, so the temperature had dropped into the upper sixties halfway through the evening, which made the party seem more festive and relieved the heat generated by her faux fur collar. She had to keep blowing the fuzz away from her mouth.

She plopped down on the chair. "I think I've officially greeted every guest for you."

"Thanks."

She did a sweep of the guests and the grill area, but no sign of Allie's husband. "Where's Stephen?"

"He had to go to work."

"What? I thought he was manning the grill."

"He handed it off to Jeremy." Allison's chin quivered. She took a drink from a plastic cup with Christmas wreaths printed on the sides. Judging by the milky substance it contained, Corinne guessed it to be egg nog. She took the cup and smelled it.

"You spiked it, didn't you?"

Allie took a sip and nodded. "Yep, and I'm not sorry for it either, because you know what? My husband's having an affair."

Corinne could tell Allie was feeling the drink. She took the cup and tossed the rest into the grass.

"Hey, I wasn't finished with that." Allie's last word slurred a bit.

How much had she drunk? She stood and tugged Allie to her feet. "Okay, let's get you inside and get some coffee in you."

As they passed the sweets table, Allie put her hand to mouth. "I think I'm going to be sick."

Allie would be mortified if she puked in front of all her guests. Corinne put her arm around Allison's waist and led her down the hall as fast as she could keep the woman moving. She thought they'd made it, but as soon as they stepped into the bedroom, Allie puked everything she drank.

All over Corinne's costume.

The Holiday Arrangement:
Chapter Four

The party had dwindled so Jeremy turned off the grill and headed back into the house. He placed the platter of burgers and hotdogs on the counter with the rest of the fixings.

Stephen still hadn't returned. And he hadn't seen Allison since Stephen told her he had to go to work and she stomped off to a table to sit alone. Not the party she hoped for. He sent a text to Stephen to tell him the party had ended, but he didn't reply. Must be buried in the paperwork he mentioned.

"Hey there." Cori stood on the other side of the counter, no longer dressed in her costume.

He pocketed his phone. "Well, hey there, Mrs. Claus." He noticed her red shirt and leaned over the counter. Black capris and sandals. "Not Mrs. Claus."

Cori slid onto one of the barstools. "Allison and egg nog do not get along."

"Isn't she lactose intolerant?"

"It would seem so. I don't think she'll get her rental deposits back on either costume."

He grimaced. "Is she okay?"

"She's sleeping it off."

"Spiked too?"

"Yep."

Their banter hadn't changed, despite the years that had passed. Jeremy remembered loving that aspect of their relationship.

Several people walked by the kitchen, waving and thanking Jeremy for the great burgers and dogs before they left.

Cori watched them leave before turning back around. "Well done, Santa. You throw a great party."

"Yeah, not bad for a guy who only planned to stay for hors d'oeuvre."

"Parties still not your thing?" She did a half-smile and half-frown thing with her lips.

"Not really." He laughed. She remembered that about him?

"I know what you mean." She raised her brows as she popped a piece of cheese into her mouth. "I'm starved." She looked at the scraps left on the meat platter.

"I can fire the grill up again if you want a hot dog. I know there's more of those."

"No, don't bother. I'll eat at home." She scanned the area. "Is Stephen back yet?"

"No. And he isn't answering my text."

She gave him a concerned look. "Everyone's gone. I don't want to leave food while Allie's passed out."

"Tell you what, help me get the food put away and I'll reward you with dinner at this little place I know out on the beach."

She tilted her head in thought.

He really wanted her to say 'yes' and step back into the past, just a little, with the guy she used to call her best friend.

They cleaned the place up in record time. Corinne was impressed by how well they worked together. She tackled the food table while he took care of collecting all the plates and cups.

Three giant garbage bags and an hour later, the place appeared back to normal. Aside from the explosion of Christmas decorations covering most of the house and a refrigerator maxed to the gills with leftovers. Allie could deal with all that later.

Since she didn't want to leave her car behind, she followed Jeremy to the place he mentioned. Some new place that just opened in the village. As she drove over the bridge onto Siesta Key, a slew of memories flooded her mind.

Hanging out with friends at the beach or the movies. Doing homework together—he helped her with math, she helped him with English. Then the graduation party—she'd shown up late and found Jeremy sitting by himself.

They blew off the party and went for a walk down the beach. Something had felt off about him that night, but he never opened up. So she chalked it up the realization that they'd soon be in different parts of the country for college.

A tap on the window brought her back to reality. Jeremy stood outside her door, smiling his familiar grin. How long has she sat here, lost in the past? She opened the door. "Sorry. Guess I have a lot on my mind."

His smile slid a bit. "Everything okay?"

"Yeah, I'm good. Just remembering the past a bit. I only moved back about a month ago and haven't had time to hit the beach yet."

He opened the door to the restaurant releasing a steady buzz of voices and the tantalizing aromas of grilled foods into the night. Her stomach jumped to full alert as she realized she'd eaten almost nothing at Allie's party.

"Wow, my mouth is already filling with saliva just from the smell."

Jeremy laughed.

She did a sudden intake of her breath. "Did I really say that? Is that TMI?"

"Not at all. You haven't changed much, Cori." The hostess led them to a booth near the back.

She slid in the far side so as to face the front of the restaurant—a habit she'd learned from going out with Peter. Best to have the exit scoped out in case he drank too much and started making a scene. She actually couldn't remember the last time she went out and relaxed at a restaurant.

And she had to admit, she breathed a sigh of relief when he ordered only iced tea when their server came to take their drink orders.

"Cori?"

"Oh, sorry. Lost in thought again." She grabbed the menu and mentally shook herself to stay in the present.

Jeremy set his menu aside. "I noticed Allison calls you by your full first name. Do you not use your nickname anymore?"

Dinner choice made, she set her menu on top of his. How did she answer that question without giving him information about her past that she'd rather not share? "Not really. I guess after college most people just called me Corinne and it stuck."

Why tell him that Peter didn't like her nickname and wanted her to use her full appropriate name. Nicknames were for children.

"Should I stop calling you Cori then?"

He stared at her with those gray-green eyes, as if he could see right into the very heart of her existence. Some things didn't change, or need to for that matter. "No, I like it when you call me Cori." She felt her cheeks heat up a bit and silently thanked the server for showing up with the water pitcher.

She always felt safe, like someone had her back when he gave her that slow smile.

Just like he did now...

Grab your copy...
vinci-books.com/holidayarrangement

About the Author

Dineen Miller is an Amazon bestselling and award-winning author of both fiction and nonfiction, but only recently discovered she has a sublime addiction to writing and reading romantic comedies. In addition to these, she's been known to write romantic suspense and has dabbled with thrillers and fantasy.

Needing additional outlets for her creativity, she's designed several coloring books under her own name and under Hue Manatee Art, and has crocheted too many afghans to count. No, she does not have cats, but she is a dog-mom to two furry rescues that answer to wiggle butt and snuggle boy. And she's married to a punny guy, who thinks she's unique.